I0783515

Published by John E. Johnson
June 2025

THE JILTED RANCHER

And Other Collected Short Stories

John E. Johnson

TABLE OF CONTENTS

THE JILTED RANCHER

1

She would always remember the first and only time she'd seen him in person on stage at his solo concert in Colorado Springs, when his bow across the strings had seemed to grab onto her and draw her in. Every note had found a way to escape the room to either glide way up over the Rockies or cry through the tall pines on the mountainside, telling a mournful story of some unimaginable sorrow from deep within him, some private place known only to him.

Her tearful eyes had overflowed from the haunting and lonesome violin tunes he played. She had ever-so-discretely dabbed at her moist eyes with a neatly pressed white handkerchief and really worried that someone might notice. And she would be mortified if her girlfriends, Minnie and Opal, made mention of it during the intermission or when the concert would be over later that evening. They just might join her to swarm up onto the stage at the very end to get their programs autographed by the young violinist as she intended to do. She really hoped they would.

Marjora had fully expected more haunting and heart-breaking Baroque music throughout the 2nd half, but to everyone's surprise, Mr. Gene Johnson, the blue-eyed rancher with the curly blond hair, started the set with a rousing Paganini composition that brought the house down from the sheer energy and volume of the piece. She was the first to react with a loud shriek before others in the room began to clap with real enthusiasm.

Oh, how she loved that man from out on the plains! She knew he could never really be hers, of course, but a girl of only 22 years of age who had just recently emerged from those Roaring Twenties could at least have him in her dreams, couldn't she?

He would always remember the first time he saw and heard her as well. That excited shriek had come from the middle of the 2nd row, from that female with the round, horn-rimmed glasses and the perfectly waved dark brown hair, the girl with that ear-to-ear grin that beamed at him amid the thunderous applause from the rest of the audience.

He decided to rearrange the next set to include a few more fast-paced works. He fully intended to give the audience more of what they had so strongly reacted to and still manage to keep an eye on his most ardent admirer, the young lady who was seemingly so lost in his music.

The program closed with a return to the slow and mournful notes that spilled out from his violin, truly beautiful yet woebegone music that told even more heart-wrenching scenarios that most concertgoers would probably know, like the sad longing expressed in "Oh, Shenandoah," followed by a brand-new song from 1913 called "Danny Boy," that sorrowful tune that most folks could somehow relate to.

And to Marjora Benefiel, who by now was constantly dabbing at her tear brimmed eyes, it seemed that the dashing bow-tied violinist was playing just for her.

As it turned out, he might as well have been since his world had been completely ripped apart just 1 week earlier during the summer of 1932. There was no one left to play for anymore, so he would hang up his bow for the very last time later that night out at the ranch house.

2

Early in 1909, John David Johnson had heard of the newest government offer referred to as the Enlarged Homestead Act that would double the total number of free acres of land to be lived on and "proved up" over 1 continuous 5-year period. He decided to take full advantage of this truly unbelievable government giveaway and moved his family out from Humphreys, Missouri to the eastern plains of Colorado to claim an entire section of this raw land. The large farm he had liquidated at auction yielded enough cash that, when added to what he had saved from his law practice, enabled him to build a farmhouse along with a barn and still allow for the purchase of 15 head of cattle to range across 640 acres. Barbed wire, fence posts, corn seed, and a few chickens completed the ranch.

Knowing that he would be exchanging rich Midwest farmland that generally had adequate rainfall for the extremely dry climate way out west, he had listened carefully to reports about how to locate water on the dry plains. Apparently, those characterized as strictly dry-land farmers had little choice but to rely on the psalmist's clearly written observation, "He watereth the hills from His chambers." But various locals had modified that passage somewhat to meet their more immediate needs, turning it into a prayer of pleading, a prayer that sounded more like, "Wilt Thou not now also water the *plains* from Your chambers?"

He had heard that strong southwest winds powered what ranchers called a windmill to draw water from underground if a well was dug deep enough. And J.D. Johnson had managed to retain enough cash money to do just that—have 2 sufficiently deep wells, each with one of those windmills that would soon dot the ranchlands below the Front Range.

Gene was the oldest of the 5 Johnson boys and was already 14 by the time the first crop of pinto beans was ready to harvest during the fall of 1911. He had adapted well to farming and the ranch life in general, demonstrating a really good work ethic along with boundless energy. Everyone around noticed that he was constantly whistling as he worked on the place, with the tunes being easily recognizable as classical ones. Yes, everyone noticed.

He had started playing the violin at 6 years of age and had shown a natural ability with the instrument. The violin had been handed down to him by an uncle who had patiently worked with the boy to ease out his truly unbelievable sense of scales and notes and the delicate ways to work with the bow. And by the time he was a young man of 18 in Colorado, most of his spare time would be spent with a violin. He could be found each evening after supper sitting in the barn or, in deep midwinter, up in the corner of an upstairs bedroom, producing soothing and sometimes even haunting tunes while at other times romping on the instrument in a fast and furious manner.

While his persistent violin playing very often irritated his younger brothers, both of his parents, J.D. and May, always defended Gene and even encouraged the other boys to show interest in at least learning to play the piano, the old upright one that sat up against the wall by the west-facing window that framed an excellent view of Pikes Peak off in the distance. But that would not materialize, since it quickly became obvious that only Gene had any interest in making music. His mother did know the piano, though. She would open an old Methodist hymnal every Sunday afternoon soon after the mid-day dinner and dessert had been served. Her oldest son would stand on the right side of the bench and use his bow to soften the piano notes as he gazed out at the distant mountain that rose to 14,000 feet.

They would most often play for close to a full hour, with May singing the words to "Softly and Tenderly" before finishing the family's Sunday singalong with her cherished "Sweet Hour of Prayer," which usually produced a request from Mr. Johnson for an encore as he sat in silence in his big overstuffed chair by the fireplace, his head tilted back, his eyes always closed, and his fingers interwoven as his hands rested atop his bald head.

Each of Gene's brothers, Marcus, Poole, Wayne, and even the youngest one, Hermit, accepted this Sunday afternoon "service" within their own front room with reluctance. Really? Hadn't the buckboard ride down to Ellicott for attendance at the Sunday school hour followed by an hour or so of the preaching time been enough religion for 1 day? Apparently not. It was one thing to endure a sacred music hour within the home when those fierce chinook winds swooped down off the Front Range of the Rockies and piled up drifted snowbanks that covered all the roads. Not a single soul would dare to venture out for any travel in such impossible conditions. Besides, the building used for church services would be buttoned up tight anyway, so church would have to be missed.

But this—right in the middle of a beautiful summer Sunday afternoon, no less? Some things just seemed so wrong to these young Johnson men who, dressed in starched white shirts on their only day off, would much rather be out on horseback sparking the young ladies from the neighboring ranches or spending the afternoon tossing a baseball back and forth out in the front yard.

3

The Sutherlands from Ohio had established their new home on El Paso Boulevard in Manitou Springs during the summer of 1913 and had soon felt right at home in the high elevation of the small town. Clifford, the middle son from this prosperous family, and his wife, Eunice, desired a ranch for raising horses, though, so they moved down from the mountains to the wide-open plains near Peyton, Colorado. With no children, their beloved horses became their life.

It was to this Colorado ranch that their first cousin, Matilda Sutherland, had traveled out from Cleveland by train during the last 2 summers to live the life of a carefree cowgirl and to ride Duke, the gray stallion, at rather breakneck speeds along the country roads. She would ride Duke at precisely 12 noon every day, including Sundays, and soon become known among all the nearby ranchers as that 30-year-old summer visitor who easily matched the high-spiritedness of the horse she loved.

What an amazing spectacle she made with her blond ponytail flying out from behind her as Duke's hooves thundered across the prairie!

Suitors would go calling at the ranch house from time to time and would immediately discover her natural beauty and sophisticated charm. Some of the young men would feel intimidated by this very beautiful and powerful young woman packaged in such a small and delicate frame. Still others mustered enough courage to invite her out for a picnic on a Saturday afternoon down at the reservoir on old man Kilmer's farm that served as the community swimming hole, or even for a dinner on the grounds after a Sunday service, but every invitation would always be politely declined.

Millie basked in the fawning attention given her by the area ranchers, of course. She would always smile brightly and even participate in warm conversation, but any real return of affection seemed to the men to be more than just a little reserved. Instead, it was downright illusive.

She wasn't the typical Colorado cowgirl that any of them had known, not by a long shot, leaving them to wonder about her life in Cleveland. Was she already married to a man back in Ohio who was too busy with business affairs to join her out West? But if so, where were her wedding rings? Maybe she was betrothed to another but chose not to disclose it. Whatever the real reasons for her arms-length social interactions with all the men of eastern Colorado, it did little to prevent their constant, earnest pursuit of *her*. Pure braggadocio as well as outrageous back-door wagers were part of this contest to see who could win this Summer Queen of the Great Plains.

Gene was certainly aware of Miss Millie as well. What red-blooded man working outside on his place could miss seeing her as she flashed by on horseback? And he had heard much of the talk about how she had always played hard-to-get, since the general stores in Peyton and Ellicott and even out at Calhan buzzed with real speculation and wonder about this sweet young lady from Cleveland.

Gene Johnson, like his father, was highly respected by all the folks out on the eastern ranchlands in the early 1930s, so it may well have been inevitable that he would be selected. This high regard stemmed, at least in some part, from his perfectly straight row crops and the overall appearance of his ranch, where federal government-issued red cedars—"the scourge of the prairie" to some purists—followed the line of the seasonal creek out on the west side and formed a perfect windbreak to safeguard the topsoil. Stately Lombardy poplars lined both sides of the long, wide driveway leading up to the house that was always kept freshly painted.

Despite blinding dust storms that often rolled across the prairie because of the historic drought during all those Great Depression years, Gene's place seemed to withstand the severe onslaught better than many other spreads out on the open, barren plains. And his rigid determination to always offer fair prices for his produce, hogs, and meat butchering services, along with his honest appraisal of any farmland acreage that occasionally came up for resale, also served to bolster his good reputation. He was rightfully proud of being considered trustworthy.

So, it really did seem almost inevitable. After all, this available 35-year-old man was quite good looking, and he was friendly to everyone he encountered. He was constantly whistling, as if cheerfulness somehow came naturally for him. And he was a violinist as well, an accomplished one who played with the Colorado Springs Ensemble each Saturday evening during the summer months.

According to his many bachelor friends, this made him the perfect candidate—the exact gentleman to claim Millie once and for all.

Each friend offered his very best advice about how to approach this conquest. Gene was certainly aware of every turn-down that had occurred over the last 2 summers, so was skeptical of most suggestions. Carl, though, pointed out that no one had yet approached her with a large bouquet of red roses, for example. Wade offered that a fresh cake, prepared especially for Millie by his mother, had not yet been presented.

But it was a perfect suggestion from his own brother that prompted him to start seriously calculating how he would take on this exciting challenge. Poole had reminded him that he owned a young stallion, the glistening black 3-year-old colt he had named Raider that was kept in the back pasture. Raider did not get ridden every single day, but he did get plenty of daily exercise, since that beautiful horse could usually be seen galloping around the pasture simply to let off excess energy.

A winning strategy had been devised! Raider would now be ridden every day for the next several weeks to prepare for the upcoming race, one that neither Millie nor any of the ranchers knew anything about. The brothers intended to keep it that way.

On the scheduled date and time selected for this contest, Saturday, June 25th, 1932, right at 12:30 PM, Poole swung open the wide gate on the back pasture and out rode Gene and Raider, making the extreme right-hand turn onto the dirt road that headed south toward Ellicott and gunning it as they heard the loud approach of Millie astride Duke.

Who was this mysterious rider on that black stallion, anyway? Who was this horse that was running stride for stride with Duke? And how could it possibly be true that this inside horse was gradually pulling away by a head, now by 2, with the rider seemingly prone with only his curly blond hair blowing behind him?

When they reached the outskirts of Ellicott, they rose in the saddles to allow the horses to settle into a trot, then a brisk walk during the last quarter mile before pulling up under the shade cast by a small cluster of cottonwood trees.

There they met for the very first time. They gazed deeply into the blue eyes of each other, completely taken with the face and person astride the horse next to them.

Has anyone heard of love at first sight?

Does anyone even believe it?

4

Never in the collective memory of all the Colorado ranching folks living on the plains had any courtship and subsequent engagement been so exceptionally brief. And neither had anyone ever witnessed such an immediate and intense love between a man and a woman, unless, of course, they would privately rank their own personal romance in the same way that Millie and Gene modeled true love.

The Drennan schoolhouse in Ellicott was selected as the very best location to hold the wedding. One of the little classrooms would serve as the chapel, and the traveling Methodist preacher would officiate the exchanging of the vows at precisely 3:00 PM on the 3rd Saturday of August in 1932. The 2nd classroom would be decorated for the reception immediately following the ceremony, with a large red banner on the wall stating August 20th with the couple's names written in calligraphy across the top. A rendering of the 2 thoroughbreds racing across the open plains would be depicted along the bottom of the banner, and a towering wedding cake baked by none other than Grammy Johnson, whose cakes had long been the standard for quality and elegance throughout the entire region, would rest on the white-draped table taking center stage.

Cliff and Eunice Sutherland and all the area Johnsons had fully thrown themselves into the arrangements for the most spectacular social event of the summer. And that date was fast approaching, with just under 1 week before the ceremonial wedding bells would start ringing.

Everyone had somehow already heard that neither the Sutherlands from Manitou Springs nor those in Cleveland would be attending the wedding—there was just way too much bad blood between those 2 families—but the friends and relatives of the groom would completely fill the school classroom that was to substitute for a wedding chapel when the day and hour arrived, a glorious day coming up on Saturday.

"Why are you still so jumpy, Gene? Would you just stop that infernal fidgeting? I really do have the ring right here in my right-hand pocket."

The encouragement from his best man was certainly well intentioned, and he really did appreciate all the special attention, but still. This getting married was proving to be a lot more nerve-wracking than he had imagined. Surely Poole remembered how awkward he had felt just a couple of years earlier when Gene stood up for him when he and Rhoda had tied the knot. But now, with those roles reversed, he just couldn't stop adjusting his collar as he wondered if his tie was centered. He constantly felt the need to shift around inside his suit jacket that he thought was ill-fitting. Even worse, he couldn't stop worrying if his pants, sporting that new-fangled fly fastener, were even properly zipped. Oh, yes, he was pretty much a wreck!

"Hey, there, big brother," Poole continued, "You look very good in that wedding outfit. Handsome, really. And you can relax now. It's time. You know I've got your back."

Reverend Lloyd Matthews beckoned first for Gene, then Poole to follow behind him as he headed out to initially stand over on the right side of the improvised platform centered in front of the folding chairs that held the wedding guests.

The room was completely packed! There weren't any available chairs except on the very front row where Cliff and his wife Eunice would be seated during the ceremony. Mrs. Ophelia Grundy was already at the piano, just waiting for the nod from the officiating clergyman to begin the prelude that would allow the bridesmaid to enter the chapel before the traditional wedding march would commence.

Gene really did cut an impressive figure as he stood watching the back entrance door, his face incredibly tanned and his curly blond hair slicked back with a thick musk-scented pomade. His lovely Millie would enter on the left arm of Cliff in just a few minutes, and he felt like his heart would just burst with love for her—his soon-to-be bride!

Because the groom's eyes had been entirely focused on the door at the very back of the room, he hadn't bothered to scan the full room to locate where his parents or all his brothers were seated. And he was completely oblivious to the empty chair that should have already been occupied by Mrs. Cliff Sutherland.

But Poole had noticed. Where was Eunice? Rehearsal plans had not utilized both Cliff and Eunice to usher Millie down the aisle to join Gene up on the platform. It was odd that she was not already seated. Very odd.

When the piano finally started to play, many twisted around to catch a glimpse of the bridesmaid, Sarah Lovington, who would enter to take up her position opposite the minister. When she failed to materialize for several long minutes, folks gradually turned back toward the platform to stare, first at the Reverend, then to search the faces of both the groom and his best man. And everyone clearly saw the pianist turn to seek direction from the officiating minister. Should she just keep playing on and on? The signal was given to do just that.

Had the small bridal party been delayed somehow? Had Cliff's brand new 1932 Ford failed to start up, or, more likely, had there been a flat tire?

To be sure, by this time everyone in the assembly was already imagining all kinds of scenarios—everyone except the groom. No, not Gene Johnson. He simply continued to keep his eyes glued to that door, but many seemed to stir in restlessness as each minute kept slipping away.

Poole had noticed their brother Wayne, who was seated near the back of the room, slip out the side door at the sound of rapidly approaching hoofbeats. Upon his return to the room a few minutes later, he stood in the rear doorway and met Gene's eyes, then quickly caught the gaze of his brother Poole and the Reverend Matthews before raising his left hand with an extended forefinger and making a slicing motion across his throat in that universal gesture signifying that something is abruptly over.

The clergyman called out to him to feel free to just speak right up and say what he might know about the situation. Then the piano suddenly stopped. Wayne quickly made his way to the front of the chapel room without making eye contact with anyone. Abruptly turning to face the assembled guests, he blurted out,

"Darrell, you all know Darrell Cates, that foreman out at the Sutherland's . . . well, he just rode down here to say there isn't going to be any wedding at all. He said Millie is in the Springs and has already boarded the overnight train that heads back to Cleveland!"

The room erupted in gasps and moans. Gene clearly heard his mother's sobs from the front row down on his left. He also heard a distinct hissing sound that his father often made through his clinched teeth when something really irritated him.

Still standing with his gaze frozen on the doorway in absolute disbelief, his face no longer tan but bright red, Gene had to be escorted, almost pulled off the platform by his 2 brothers while the minister went on and on, using soft words intended to help soothe the jilted groom's emotions and maybe help keep him all together. Both Poole and Wayne knew that all those soothing words were not even being heard by their destroyed brother, and they wanted Rev. Matthews to be quiet. There was simply nothing to say anyway, so they wanted him to give it up. Probably giving him the customary gratuity would get him to leave them alone and head out on his way. They could only hope as much as Poole slipped the bill into the parson's outreached hand.

Gene had poured out his complete heart.

Millie had completely wasted it.

The destruction of Gene Johnson would be epic—would anyone even dare to discuss it out loud? Oh, his mother, May, had tried to console him back in the little anteroom afterwards, but it was of little to no avail. Reminding him that so very little was known about Millie, after all, and that the whole thing had been so rushed was a viewpoint that was certainly not shared by Gene. He insisted that he knew her, he *really* knew her well, and that their special love was much more genuine than that of any other couple.

His brothers drove him from the wedding venue out to his ranch and all offered well-intentioned but still quite awkward condolences, expressions like those offered at any funeral. Both Poole and Wayne had lingered with Gene for about a quarter-hour longer than Marcus and Hermit had as they all waited for their parents to arrive, but there were ranch chores of their own to get to, so they, too, had to slip away when they heard the car in the driveway.

Grampy and Grammy Johnson arrived after having spent time helping in the breakdown of the reception room. The huge wedding cake had been donated to a family with 6 children; it would not go to waste. The large banner had been ripped into pieces and hauled away, since no one, especially Gene or anyone else in his immediate family, would ever want to lay eyes on it again. All the wedding gifts were placed on the car's back seat for eventual return.

When his mother entered the ranch house, his father went straight out to the barn to handle the general chores that needed to be attended to—the animals had to be fed on time and fresh water needed to be pumped. Besides, he really had no idea what to say to his grieving son who had been so awkwardly and publicly humiliated. J.D. wasn't a very demonstrative man. Displays or even simple expressions of affection were not part of his personality, so what could he possibly say that would help Gene?

Since he was at a complete loss for what to do for his hurting son, he lingered an unnecessarily long time over the ranch chores, just wanting this whole thing to be over. He knew none of the Johnsons would ever be able to forget this horrible date in August of 1932. And even the literal day of the month, the 20th, would probably live on in infamy.

By the time J.D. gained the courage to step inside the house, he found them seated at the kitchen table where Gene was slowly eating a plate of scrambled eggs and day-old biscuits. Gene turned his hollowed eyes toward the location where his father stood, but since neither of them found anything to say to each other, he continued to slowly work on the food his mother had prepared. After he had finished the last bite and sipped the cool water from the aluminum tumbler in his hand, he then turned to face his father, bracing himself so his voice wouldn't break,

"I can't believe it. I just can't. I can't believe Millie has done this to me!"

Grampy made that all-familiar hissing sound with his teeth before responding. When he eventually spoke, his words were measured but warm and very softly uttered in something close to a whisper,

"You just come over to our place to stay, Gene. You shouldn't even be here right now. Come on. You get in the car with us. We'll make room. We'll head over there right away. And we can come back over here another day to gather some of your things."

They rode in silence for the entire 11 miles out to the old home place. The jilted groom sat staring out the passenger window with his hands folded across his lap, watching the prairie as it rolled by in the failing evening light. He knew every slight rise and every little gully, and he knew exactly where each cluster of rabbit brush would appear alongside the road. His mother stared straight ahead while wedged in the middle, her new dress pulled way up to the knees to accommodate the long gear shift sticking up from the floor. And Mr. Johnson, too, focused only on the road ahead, occasionally stealing a sideways view of his son, using the need to swerve to avoid a rut in the dirt road as a reason for turning his head at all.

"What happened to just scare her off like that? I must have done something wrong. So very wrong," Gene sobbed, "But what was it?"

He didn't give his parents sufficient time to respond before continuing,

"Why couldn't I see this whole thing coming? I *knew* her. And I *loved* her, Dad." He wiped at his eyes and runny nose with his shirtsleeve and then sputtered on, "On our wedding day she took the train back to Ohio! Really? So *now*," he wailed, "what? Just what am I supposed to do *now*?"

Raised in an era when grown men weren't supposed to show all that much emotion and certainly to never cry, Gene was breaking all those rules as the 3 sat out in the front room. While his father was extremely uncomfortable with his son's uncontrolled feelings of total rejection, his mother, in a way, did seem better equipped to deal with his breakdown. But both knew to allow him to continue venting his total humiliation and deep grief, so they made no attempt to interrupt him nor try to answer those questions that simply had no answers.

Finally, his father rose from his chair and walked over to the cabinet opposite the fireplace, returning with 2 glasses and a nearly full bottle of bourbon that he always kept there.

"Here, Gene. This awful, awful circumstance calls for a glass of strong drink right about now."

He measured out 3-fingers for each glass, avoiding what would most likely be a glare of total disapproval on his wife's face. But May knew that this would not be the time to raise any real objection to the "devil's brew" being consumed in her own house. Instead, she surprised both the men by asking for just a little touch for herself.

Gradually the heartache that they each felt wound down enough for Gene to say that he just wanted to turn in. His mother directed him up to his old room, where the sheets were clean and ready for use. Gene managed to mumble a "goodnight" and disappeared up the stairs into his familiar bedroom that was still furnished exactly as it had always been. Sleep came quickly, a rather restless, deeply disturbed sleep with unpleasant dreams that he was unable to recall by the first light of morning.

Massaging the base of his neck, he now regretted the whiskey from the night before only because his head was splitting. But at the time, he knew his father was right to find a way to help ease the unbelievable pain that he had been wallowing in. And it had worked.

It was now Sunday morning, but Gene had no plans whatsoever to attend a church service. He knew his parents wouldn't show themselves in church, either. Not that any one of them was having a crisis of faith, neither a thought that there might have been some divine abandonment of Gene. It was nowhere near that complicated; it was really nothing more than a feeling of unbelievable humiliation.

No, this Johnson family would not be darkening the doorway of any church. Not on this Sunday. Not any Sunday for a while. It was just way too soon.

Instead, they would begin the day with big mugs of strong boiled coffee over a hearty country breakfast that would include slices of Grammy's apricot-filled coffee cake drizzled with almond-flavored icing.

There was something overshadowing the damaged man that had to be dealt with; it just could not wait. It was his mother who employed gentle persuasion to help Gene understand how critically important it really was.

The end of the summer-long concert season for the Colorado Springs String Ensemble, locally referred to as the Saturday Strings, was already scheduled with a final presentation coming up on Saturday evening. A strictly solo performance by the very talented local violinist, Mr. Gene Johnson, aptly billed as "The Blue-Eyed Rancher with the Curly Blond Hair," would be featured, with the programs announcing this Grand Finale already printed. May had been informed that all concert tickets had completely sold out. While his mother acknowledged that Gene had suffered a very tragic blow, she assured him that every ticketholder would be totally unaware of any of it. Besides, to her way of thinking, life, even after emotional death, still goes on. She maintained that this final event of the summer season must proceed as scheduled. There was just no escaping it.

Gene wrestled for a few days over his decision about performing Saturday night. Finally convinced that it would be highly unlikely that even a single person in attendance would know about his awful jilting from the previous Saturday afternoon, he surrendered to the already-programmed event. He did have to keep shaking off a sense of impending stage fright, though, since he was more than a little worried that what he had totally conquered so long ago just might come creeping back around his door. Knowing that he was a real emotional wreck, something like that could trip him up if he didn't stay on guard.

Without telling anyone, he knew that this would be his very last public violin concert—Gene's final page. He was certain that he wouldn't be able to serenade anyone again, including himself, because too much joy had drained out of him while standing up at the altar waiting for Millie to show up, only to have her totally disappear on him.

But this last hurrah would be tackled with all that he had left, using every trace of natural ability, training, and artistic nuance that he could draw from. Concert guests would deserve that much.

The concert hall was abuzz with soft chatter until the lights started to fade to all black. When the curtains drew back, the violinist was standing in a bright circle of light with no music stand placed before him. Huge applause of greeting filled the auditorium. Gene then deeply bowed, twice, before drawing up his bow to begin playing.

Later, during the intermission, Gene quickly vanished behind the curtain. He certainly wanted to avoid any engagement with anyone. But backstage, Orvis, the curtain operator, somehow did manage to find him. The gentleman, in his thick Scottish brogue, lavished the violinist with praise for an outstanding concert. And Gene admitted to himself that he, too, felt like he had indeed performed very, very well.

When the concert finally resumed, he fairly romped on a selection of his favorite Paganini compositions. The crowded room came alive with applause and real adoration. Gene could feel the genuine love from the guests—he really could—and that love gave him an extraordinary sense of energy to continue playing.

He had reserved 2 very special tunes just in case the audience demanded an encore, which they certainly had. Knowing it was the last public venue he would ever play, he poured himself into 2 very sad songs to round out the evening's program: "Oh, Shenandoah" immediately followed by "Danny Boy."

Since he was still bowing to the deafening applause, he didn't initially notice when a few program-waving attendees rushed up onto the platform and pleaded for autographs. Among them was the girl that he had been watching throughout most of his performance. Trying very hard to avoid panicking, he worried about Orvis. Where *was* he? Why hadn't he already pulled the curtain closed? Now it was too late, and he felt trapped.

Gathering every single ounce of remaining strength, Gene smiled as he asked for everyone's name before signing the individual programs.

"My name is Marjora," she gushed, "and I absolutely love you . . . and your violin music. What a concert!"

"Well, thank you, Marjora. Thanks so much. Now just how is your name spelled?"

As he began to autograph the front of her program, she blurted out not only the way to spell her name but also that she lived nearby, in Colorado Springs, only 2 blocks over at 312 Cheyenne Boulevard at the top of the street.

Gene felt color rising in his face as he smiled at her while lasering in on her deep brown eyes. He really couldn't think of any response to what seemed to him to be an on-the-spot invitation for courting her. Now he *was* panicking and needed to quickly escape.

Luckily, the final guests waiting in the line, a mother with her daughter, interrupted with a request for an autograph for the little girl. Wonderful. He was saved by a child named Julie!

After signing her wrinkled program, he managed to quickly retreat to the safety of the backstage. Finding his way down the stairs to the back exit door with his violin and bow tucked under his left arm, he headed straight across the alleyway to his parent's parked vehicle, happy to see that his father was standing outside with the driver's door wide open and his foot resting on the running board. As Gene approached, his father twisted around and reached over to the handle on the back suicide door and flung it open while exclaiming "Very good job!" Gene then literally threw the violin with its bow to the far side of the back seat before sinking into the comfort of the seat directly behind the driver.

"Oh my, Gene, that was the best you've ever played! It was truly awesome!"

Already relaxed up front in the passenger seat, his mother had turned around to heap praise upon him. Even in the limited nighttime light inside the interior of the car, he could tell that she was beaming and had really meant every word of her congratulations.

They journeyed without conversation along State Highway 24, the road out from Colorado Springs that had only recently become hard surfaced and headed northeast toward the home place. Only the singing of the narrow tires on the pavement and the sound of the engine disturbed the quiet as his father, not accustomed to nighttime driving, sat hunched over while tightly gripping onto the steering wheel in total concentration, straining to see what was only dimly illuminated by the Ford's headlamps. The occasional oncoming car with lights shining into his eyes was especially stressful. But most aggravating, by far, was the vehicle that had tailgated him for several miles before finally managing to get around the slower car.

For the first 25 miles of the drive, Gene sat in the darkness of the back seat reliving the concert as he slowly settled down from the excitement and sheer adrenalin rush that such stage performances always produced. He was quite happy with how everything had gone on stage, everything, that is, until the very end when those seeking autographs had managed to swarm up onto the platform before the curtain had closed.

There was that young woman who had so unsettled him. Was her name Margaret? Then he remembered it was a very unusual name—Marjora. What he knew for certain was that he really wanted her completely out of his mind just as desperately as he wanted any trace of Millie to leave him alone forever.

By the time they pulled off the blacktop to bounce along on the dirt road that would carry them the last several miles out to the ranch, he had already started slipping into an alarmingly dark mood that matched the darkness outside under a waning crescent moon. He found himself dwelling on the real horror of the previous Saturday, and a deep depression sprinkled with bitterness was overtaking him.

Gene had been totally destroyed and needed to find refuge—a hideout—a safe place to fall apart before his heart could ever begin to mend. And his parent's ranch would be the perfect place to do just that.

MARJORA

PROLOGUE

"I was born an aristocrat!"

The statement was expressed as a whine along with a good measure of faked weepiness. It was delivered through her clinched teeth and came from a place of bitterness rather than from disappointment alone.

Our mother imagined that a real aristocrat, someone living up to the appropriate standard, would crochet or do needlepoint as part of the town's social circles but would never have to do what *she* was required to do, to literally make, by hand no less, the clothes to put on the backs of her own family. Never. She just knew that she should not have to live this way at all.

Frustration bordering on anger could be seen in her eyes as she fumbled to rethread a sewing needle that had pricked a fingertip on her hand. The tedious work of cutting fabric and following a McCall's pattern was hard enough on any given day. But this was worse, with such poor lighting, where the only available light managed to make it through the drawn curtain at the window by the antique Singer sewing machine where she was seated. The curtain was drawn to help keep the cold air from coming into the house from around the worn-out casing of the single-paned window. The cold and the lack of adequate lighting were enough to struggle with, but the needle stick on her finger just kept throbbing away, causing her anger to only increase.

Then she just blurted it out, again,

"I was born an aristocrat!"

We had heard the same proclamation from time to time over the years, a statement that was intended to be taken very seriously by all her young children. Within earshot of her voice as we sat around on this snowy winter afternoon, we noticed, yet again, that she had no intention of ever letting Daddy hear her verbalize it. The discussion was immediately dropped when he entered the kitchen through the back door, stomping the snow from his almost completely worn-out low-rise shoes before dropping the wet firewood into the cardboard box beside the pot-bellied stove, that reliable old stove that managed to warm the back part of the long, narrow house. He then stoked the firebox with chunks of dry wood before stepping back outside for yet another load. When the door was fully closed, Gloria, or "Little Sister" to all of us, immediately raised the subject again by asking what an aristocrat even was. I then dared to ask just what made our mother claim such an outlandish status.

"Yes. We all have this same aristocratic blood from my mother's side of the family," she bragged. "We come from the best, the highest levels of genteel society, since one of my great grandfathers was none other than Samuel F. B. Morse himself, the inventor of the Morse Code. You know, the code that is still used today for the telegraph."

We had heard that information before somewhere along the way, too, and were genuinely proud to be linked with this famous man. But aristocrats? Hardly. Just one glance around the room proved that to be completely false.

We would hear this only when her coping skills were at a breaking point, at rock bottom, on days when her living circumstances just seemed too hard to bear. And who could really blame her?

Besides, who *could* cope with the never-ending dust that always settled everywhere and those filthy flies that landed on everything before flying away to buzz all around the kitchen windowpane, as if they would prefer to be outside instead of endlessly pestering her?

1

It was a long-standing clarion call, first given in the middle of the American 19th century:

"Go west, young man! Go west!"

The phrase encompassed America's profound belief in her Manifest Destiny to claim the vastness of the West. Many 1000s had heeded that call, pulling up stakes and heading out to cross the Blue Ridge and way out over the Appalachian Mountains to find new places offering genuine opportunity for themselves, either individually or for their entire families. Some had stopped off in what had become known as the great Midwest, a mostly flat area with excellent soils for planting. Still others pushed further out, reaching the Great Plains or on to the Rocky Mountains. Many of these caravans ventured down to make a new life in the warm climate of the desert Southwest.

The Oklahoma Territory, commonly just called Indian Territory, had actually become the new homeland of the Cherokees when the tragedy of that infamous Trail of Tears had finally ended. The eastern portion of this region then officially became known as the Cherokee Nation. And a brand-new little town called Bartlesville had sprung up in the same area during the 1880s and would eventually boom following the discovery of crude oil off the banks of the Caney River that flowed through the town. Phillips Petroleum Co. was then founded in 1905, an entire 2 years before actual statehood was fully attained for the Oklahoma Territory.

Harleigh Marjora was born in this little oil-rich town to Hope Flora (Morse) and Bert Blair Benefiel early in 1910. By that year, the Rockies had already started calling to Bert and just would not stop urging him to move out that way, where 2 communities along the base of the Front Range, both Colorado Springs and Denver, were already fairly large and flourishing.

Nothing about northeastern Oklahoma was all that troublesome to him except being smack dab in the middle of Tornado Alley. Maybe it was time to get away, to move "lock, stock and barrel" way up into the Colorado mountains. Cold winters and occasional blizzards would surely be preferable to tornadoes, at least to Mr. Benefiel's way of thinking.

2

Manitou Springs, Colorado, where natural mineral springs provided the healing waters that Indians in the surrounding area had consistently been drinking for centuries, had created a motto for the town that read:

"AT THE FOOT OF PIKES PEAK"

The small village of approximately 1500 inhabitants was already an established tourist town because of the mineral springs and the towering mountain with its cog railway by the time the Benefiels called the place their home in 1914.

Still merely a toddler, Marjora delighted in sitting out on the big green lawn off the front porch during the summertime holding Bessy, her favorite rag doll, and laughed away when her mother bundled her up in warm winter clothing on each birthday in February for a playtime out in the magical snow that covered the stairs leading down from the back porch. Her mother, Hope, stood close by while supervising this frosty excursion, of course, with both retreating into the warm house when the cold started to bite a little too much.

Life was good. Bert had secured the job of Chief of Police serving the small municipality and exercised direct supervision over 2 young patrolmen who had recently joined the force. And nothing *ever* really happened in Manitou Springs that needed any real intervention. The official police ledger, month after month, only registered little things, nuisance things, like the pack of stray dogs in early September last year that finally had to be rounded up, followed a month or 2 later by a break-in at someone's outside shed where the only thing that appeared to have been taken was the padlock itself.

No. Absolutely nothing ever *really* happened in the town of Manitou Springs. Nothing, that is, until it *did* happen just before daybreak on Christmas morning.

Chief Benefiel's newest patrolman, Charles Manning, had pulled Christmas duty and was quite surprised by an early morning visit from a man named Virgil who had ridden to the station to report multiple gunshots near his home down on Deer Mountain Road at the edge of Pike National Forest. The sounds had come from near his house but across the road, from the dilapidated log cabin that sat back among thick pine trees. The dwelling had become inhabited only a week earlier by that odd family that had moved in during a light snowstorm, unloading cartons of their meager belongings from the old wagon after the first whisps of smoke began curling from the stovepipe.

Virgil had been informed that they went by the name of Patterson. George, his wife Ethel, and little Tommy Patterson. The man offered nothing more.

By the time Officer Manning and Virgil dismounted and entered the little cabin through the weathered door that was wide open, it rather quickly became obvious that everything was essentially over. With no fire burning in the wood stove, it was freezing cold inside the front room. A scrappy looking Christmas tree stood in the corner with small homemade paper decorations attached but without any presents at all underneath. They glanced into the dark and empty kitchen, then walked into the only bedroom where Ethel and Tommy were lying in their beds where they both had been shot while still sleeping. The sight and unmistakable smell of death from the blood and flesh were too much for Officer Manning. He immediately retched, losing his morning coffee all over the floor and onto his boots. Then Virgil grabbed his arm and yanked him backwards, yelling,

"Let's get out of here! Now!"

The icy air outside on the front porch was precisely what would help to gather themselves together. But Mr. Manning knew their initial look around was not really completed. Not yet. Where was the man of the house, this George fellow?

They both noticed the footprints tracking through the fresh snow heading out to the stable and started in that direction. An aging black mare was standing over at the far end of the corral, silently staring them down as they approached. After loosening the wire that secured the gate, they rounded a corner where bales of hay were stacked against a small tar paper shed used for tack. There they spotted the man and the empty bottle of Jim Beam. His gun was partially covered by the nearly headless body that had fallen over from the self-inflicted shotgun blast.

Charles and Virgil saddled up and left the place, with Virgil saying he had to get home to have Christmas with his family, whether he would be able to even enjoy it now or not. Officer Manning continued up to the station, knowing with absolute certainty that he would soon be required to turn right back around and spend his Christmas Day with his fellow patrol officer, Frank, and Chief Benefiel as they began the awful process of clearing up that ghastly murder-suicide scene down at the cabin.

At the end of his shift right at 3 PM, Manning walked off the job. While Chief Benefiel was seated at his desk completing the required written report, Charles went over and handed him his badge. His hands were shaking as he did so, and in a quivering voice said that he just couldn't take it, stating that he had a 5-year-old boy of his own waiting for him to come home to celebrate Christmas. He said he would rather do hard work at the Cog Railway than to have anything at all to do with police work ever again.

His partner, Frank, then walked over to stand before the Chief's desk to declare that nothing, absolutely nothing taught at the Police Academy had prepared him for this. He would go home to Denver tomorrow.

By the final day of that Christmas week, the entire Manitou Springs Police Department had resigned. Bert did have to remain working on the job for a couple of days as he arranged for the continuation of police protection from the El Paso County Sheriff's Department. In his verbal explanation to both Sheriff Wilson and to his own wife, he maintained that he was decidedly more of a gentleman than a cop could ever be, at least in the long term. His full intention was to return to a skill that he had already mastered, the very civilized skill of finish carpentry.

Manitou Springs was terribly shaken by the absolute horror from Deer Mountain Road. Area parents were unable to adequately explain to their own children how a massacre like this could happen anywhere, let alone right here in their own town, and on such a sacred, holy, and happy day as Christmas, no less. At least schoolchildren were on holiday break until well into January and wouldn't have to listen to the whole scenario dissected, repeatedly, by their own peers.

Manitou's wide-open wound would eventually start to heal. Discussions and active remembrance would slowly fade. But none of that could begin to happen until that dreadful cabin was dealt with.

It was determined that the property was owned by a widower from up around Fort Collins who was made aware of the gory circumstances and told that the Patterson family had been squatters on his property after being evicted for nonpayment of rent down in Florence. The retired owner was perplexed. How did they end up finding his abandoned property in the first place? And they had just moved right in? He was glad to accept the town's offer to access city funds to have the entire place levelled so the acreage could return to its naturally wooded state. That was exactly how all the townsfolk wanted to deal with that awful cabin.

It didn't take long for Bert and Hope to find a house down in Colorado Springs in one of the nicer parts of town up at the top of Cheyenne Boulevard. This new home would serve as the place where Marjora would be raised during all her school years through senior graduation from Cheyenne Mountain High School in 1928.

3

Life was good once again for the Benefiels up at their new home. Bert was fortunate to have plenty of work doing what he really loved to do, which was to make wooden furniture. He was very good at it, and that reputation spread among those who could afford his beautifully crafted pieces.

Hope seemed rather well suited for raising their only child, Marjora, as a well-dressed and well-spoken girl in the Colorado city they had adopted as their own. The young lady appeared happy overall. Photographs from her childhood, whether just a family portrait or a large group setting with all her classmates, always depicted Marjora wearing an enormous hair bow, as most girls her own age did, and a smile—even though no one else wore one. Had everyone been instructed to look solemn? In one schoolwide group picture of the students taken during her 4th grade year, a total of 42 students are captured on film, but she and a younger boy are the only ones with a smile. The boy's face had only the slightest trace of a grin, and neither of their smiles are teeth-revealing. But still, had they somehow managed to break a rule from the teacher standing in the very back row, the woman with the down-turned mouth?

Marjora was quite delighted to learn that she was a direct descendant of a circuit rider preacher and that she was also related to a man who had carried the U.S. mail as a Pony Express rider, then by way of the stagecoaches, and finally on the steam locomotives. But it was her blood connection to the inventor of the Morse Code that most impressed the young girl. Her mother, whose actual maiden name was Morse, had revealed the family heritage with more than just a little touch of pride in her voice. And by the time Marjora was old enough to understand the meaning of the word, she asked,

"Momma, tell me. Does our being related by blood to that inventor, Mr. Samuel F.B. Morse, make us aristocrats?"

Her father had completely endorsed this way for her to look at her world and her place in it and he had determined to bring her up as anything but a run-of-the-mill child. No, she was special, a very special girl indeed, and he treated her as such throughout her entire childhood. But probably to her detriment, he and his wife had deliberately raised Marjora to aspire to be an active participant in the country club set of Colorado Springs, something that they had already clearly attained for themselves as they enjoyed high tea at the Broadmoor Hotel most Friday afternoons. There would be no compromise at all in this regard for their daughter. Absolutely none.

Marjora and her very best friend during their last 2 years at Cheyenne High, Lois Armet, shared almost everything, from clothes to borrowed shoes, but it was the endorsement of a little rebellion from the expected societal norms of the period that proved they were pretty much in lockstep with each other's way of thinking. By 1928 the influence of the free-spirited Flappers was everywhere, and both adopted the bobbed haircuts and much shorter dresses that announced that the "new woman" was something to be reckoned with. And this detour from what their parents had expected of them was also evidenced by the choice of young men in their lives, with both girls preferring to be escorted by the handsome but not necessarily all-that-studious types, the athletic ones, the ones who showed much less promise as future attorneys, licensed engineers or physicians like their fathers, but were instead more focused on having a good time with the girls who had already graduated from high school.

The period of depending on storefront Nickelodeon entertainment alone had been replaced by gaudy art deco picture palaces where silent movies could be seen for a 25-cent ticket. These boys always seemed to have sufficient cash money on hand to take their gals twice a week, both on Saturday afternoons and again on Sunday evenings, and they were most often attracted to the movies about real gangster crime or creepy horror shows instead of those silly comedies from Charlie Chaplin.

But it was lively dancing that Marjora most enjoyed. After all, it was still the Roaring Twenties, and "doing the Charleston" with her Saturday date always took top billing with her. Being called giddy or loose by the older generation never really seemed to bother her. Life was for living, and she intended to do just that.

Each young man who took her out to the movies or entered the dance halls with her either had his own vehicle by the late 1920s or could borrow the family "flivver," the extremely popular little 2-door Model A Coupe belonging to his father. And on the occasions when the couple would make it a double date, the rear rumble seat was a most coveted spot, but only if Colorado weather permitted.

Sometimes the girlfriends would go out to the dance halls together without having escorts or even attend weekend movie matinees together, while at other times they might sit through a symphony. Yes. Each of Marjora's chums agreed. This life was to be lived!

So, was this where the long-term plans that Bert and Hope had for their daughter start to unravel? Did it all start when just a teenager in high school and her total fascination with those Flappers? Just when *did* Marjora start to follow only what *she* desired?

It would not take long before everybody would see firsthand just how deep Marjora's streak of rebellion really ran.

4

She watched from her place on the front porch as the dust-covered Ford slowly crept up the street. A man, alone in the vehicle, kept peering through the open window as he studied the numbers attached to the mailboxes in front of each house on the opposite side of the street. His shirtsleeves were rolled up despite the crisp early December air, and his deeply tanned and muscular forearm rested on the window opening as he held a half-sheet of paper in his hand that he kept glancing at. She heard a distinct screech from the brakes as the Model A came to a stop. The man stepped out but immediately turned back to reach for something left inside on the seat which he then kept hidden behind his back as he crossed the street and angled toward her house.

Marjora's jaw dropped as she fully recognized who was heading toward her. It was that plainsman, the blue-eyed rancher with the golden violin!

Quickly rising from the chair and wrapping her shawl tightly around her arms, she ran across the winter lawn to intercept him, exclaiming,

"Mr. Gene Johnson! What, oh what are you doing at my house? And what took you so long to get here?"

"Well, good day to you, Miss Marjora," he replied. "I have something here for you."

He handed over what had been concealed behind his back, a rectangular box wrapped in shiny silver paper with a red ribbon tied around it.

"Merry Christmas!

5

The arranged dates and the letter writing campaign had started with a flurry. It was already the middle of February, and the still-secret wedding date was set for June 21st.

"When are you and your mother coming out here for my mother's help with making that dress? Will I get to see you if I'm able to come into town next Friday afternoon? Will I be allowed to escort you to church on Sunday? Did you really catch it when you sneaked in so late last Saturday night? Have you been hearing all those rumors like I have? How did you like that whopper of a fib I told Mrs. Stafford when we were at their get-together last week? Pretty clever, huh?"

"Gene, you should consider letting Daddy help make that kitchen table look really nice. And he could help with all the plastering and kalsomine painting in the bedroom. Have you had enough time to change your mind about letting him go out and work on it? I sure hope I get a long letter from you next week."

Marjora, who had just had her 23rd birthday on the 1st day of February in 1933, was ready to marry Gene, who had now chosen to only refer to her by her first name, Harleigh. She was fine with that. After all, it was her name.

But there were those among them who were not so ready for such a union, specifically Mr. and Mrs. Bert Benefiel. Just how *could* their only daughter do such a thing? She intended to marry outside of her class, to drag the Benefiel family name down to the level of scrappy dirt farmers and ranchers. And this Mr. Gene Johnson had not followed the custom of asking the father for permission to take his daughter's hand in marriage, either.

And to top it all off, those Johnsons from way out in the ranch country around Peyton and Ellicott weren't even Presbyterians! It was possible that they were people from a Christian creed of some sort, but who knew? Maybe they were all Methodists or something else that was equally weird. It all just seemed rather disgraceful, especially to Bert.

It was Hope Benefiel, however, who took the initial news of the upcoming wedding especially hard. She and Marjora had always been so close. Yes, that had definitely changed considerably when her daughter had started imitating just about everything from that outrageously silly Flapper craze. Nevertheless, Hope still felt a sense of responsibility somehow for this clear failing in her daughter's upbringing. What had it been? Had she been a bit too demanding, insisting that Benefiel ladies were to act a certain way? Or had she been way too lenient at the end by allowing such nonsensical behavior to go on inside her own family?

As for Bert, he determined that all his police training should not just go to waste. Investigations had been his specialty, so he initiated the process of finding out everything he could about this Johnson man. Who were his closest friends and associates? And just how old was this man? Did he have his own ranch, or did he only rent a property from some other rancher? And of paramount importance, did he even have any money, any real means to support his daughter?

When he shared his findings with Hope, she gasped and started weeping as he sat watching her. Then she abruptly stopped crying and inquired what could be done to stop this horrible marriage. Just how could they intervene, and how could they go about telling Marjora all the sordid details? Bert felt that they should keep quiet about all of it for the time being, since he intended to watch Gene very carefully. His reasoning was that they might not be successful in stopping the marriage. In that case, it would be unfair to burden their daughter with the information. And after all, he stated,

"She's in love with the boy!"

Hope almost screeched as she retorted,

"Yes, indeed, he's some boy at 36 years old!"

6

Marjora had sensed a strain between her father and her fiancé. It was noticeable in the way Bert looked at Gene by a glance that was really more like a stare and seemed to be one of general disapproval, even if nothing had specifically been said or even discussed, let alone argued about. So, what was this all about? She'd asked Gene, but he had brushed it off, claiming that her daddy just didn't want to lose his little girl. And that was all. Could you blame him?

Why was Gene steadfastly refusing any help that her father was offering? Marjora had already seen the old ranch house that Gene would be renting for $55 for the entire year from his brother Marcus who had married and then moved away to Vermont to run his father-in-law's store. Anyone could readily see that the place needed a lot of work to make it decent for setting up housekeeping. There were no curtains at the windows; only miscellaneous pieces of mostly mismatched furniture could be found in any of the rooms. Missing was a couch for the front room. Two dusty side chairs, each upholstered in a bright green floral pattern, were all that were in that room. She had opened every door in search of indoor plumbing, but none had been found. The single bedroom was missing the bedstead, mattress, and dresser, and was also lacking the plaster that the walls in each of the other rooms had. The kitchen still had a very small but sturdy dining table with 4 matching chairs. It only needed to be sanded and stained or just painted, but otherwise it was serviceable.

So why all the reluctance to accept any help from the Benefiels? Was Gene revealing a new side of himself, a prideful side, a false pride that he intended to hide behind and just pass off as independence? Or maybe it was just plain stubbornness. Marjora intended to figure it out.

Finally, in early May, she approached her father and asked him about his thoughts regarding Gene's rigid determination to do all the necessary work himself. The reply she heard was quite troubling. While not revealing all that he had learned about this man she intended to marry, he did implore her to reconsider hitching her wagon to this rancher. He spoke with her in the same calm, even voice that he had always used to communicate with her, the same measured voice with no scold whatsoever in his tone.

Foremost among her father's concerns was that this man had no money anymore while vaguely implying that probably he once did. He successfully skirted around the real story behind the man's total collapse following that sensational jilting from last August. He desperately wanted to tell her every detail that he had uncovered, to tell her that even his own family was clearly opposed to this marriage, believing that it was coming way too soon since he was just now attempting to fully emerge from the extremely dark place where he had been wallowing. He wanted to tell her that one of his brothers had specifically said that he was not really over the girl who had left him standing at the altar, the same brother who had said that he was making a determined effort to erase her memory by taking on a new bride, and that he was acting on the rebound from a failed love.

Bert had amazing control during the conversation, but Marjora could read her father very well, and felt that there was something more, maybe something major that she was not being told, and she wondered why. Nevertheless, she was expected to believe that Gene was reluctant to accept any help at all from her daddy due to cultural differences, differences that he must certainly feel between people of "our station" compared to his "country" folks who, during this deep Depression, could really benefit from help from the well-to-do Benefiels.

Her father had pleaded with her about "hitching her wagon to this rancher," imploring her to reconsider. But why? The real reason was not being revealed.

Now she felt an overwhelming need to understand why Gene never played the violin anymore. Marjora had fallen madly in love with this man while he was performing during the concert last August. Where had that man gone? Another question-and-answer session with her fiancé was not only necessary but overdue.

Choosing to conduct this interrogation somewhere away from her home, Marjora suggested that they spend the next Saturday afternoon at the Cheyenne Mountain Zoo, a place that she had loved since it first opened during her high school years. She planned to begin "the talk" by the monkey and ape enclosure. She knew of a stone bench that was a bit elevated from the viewing area; it would offer some privacy from the noisy crowd of families pressed as close as possible to the animal cages, where children would giggle at the playfulness of the family of chimpanzees and then shriek at the occasional nastiness of one of the male apes who just might decide to spit water onto the closest viewers.

Marjora didn't waste any time or mince any words as she started. The very first question was a direct one to get the conversation rolling,

"So, Mr. blue-eyed, curly-haired—what's left of it, at least—Gene Johnson, why don't you play the violin anymore?"

She immediately sensed his bristling at that question. He didn't exactly stammer out his response, but the answer seemed sloppy and certainly did not ring with sincerity. He would not look at her, choosing instead to gaze off over the heads of the crowd below as if he was remembering back to when he last played. Was his expression one of real pain? It seemed so to Marjora.

"I just grew out of it, I guess," he finally replied. "I started when I was only 6 years old, and I've just had enough of it. Enough."

"But you are so good at it, Gene! I especially love the beautiful, haunting Baroque sounds. Someone with such incredible talent who can play like you do, and straight from the heart without even looking at the written notes, should never stop playing! Never!"

Marjora would have kept pressing on, but she saw that his face had reddened, and he was still refusing to even look at her. He was clearly shutting her out. But why? Would this be the way he would discuss things going forward in their marriage? That very thought was bouncing around in her mind and it really disturbed her. She could only guess at what had caused him to just up and quit playing. Surely something had happened. But what could it have been? Deciding to move on to yet another question that needed to be addressed and responded to—and honestly, this time—she prodded,

"Gene, tell me the real reason you won't let daddy help with the work to get the house ready in time for our wedding? We're running out of time!"

She wasn't prepared for his immediate reaction. He swirled around on the bench to directly face her with an angry look in his eyes that startled her. His temper seemed to flare, and his voice rose as he responded. What he said hurt her deeply.

"I cannot work with a person like him! I just can't do it," he continued, "He had no right to do what he did. No man has a right to do that. No right at all."

Marjora was shocked to hear his words and volume. She was now quite subdued. No one had ever spoken to her in such a loud and harsh tone. No one.

The hurt sounded in her voice as she asked him what he was even talking about. What had her father done to make him so angry? And why was he raising his voice at her? These questions flowed from her while tears were forming in her eyes.

"You want to know what he did? Well, okay then, I'll tell you. That daddy of yours drove out to Peyton and Ellicott and started nosing all around and asking all kinds of questions about me." His voice got even louder. "And really personal questions, too, like if I had any way of making a living. He asked if I was just living off my parents by tending to the hogs and all."

His voice had become so loud that several people at the rear of the crowd below them had turned around to catch a peek at the man up on the bench. But Gene didn't even notice. His rant kept going,

"He talked to folks all around out there and asked them who my closest contacts were. Someone saw him driving away from the Sutherland horse ranch where he must have been asking lots of questions. No doubt about that!

He showed up out at my brother's farm, too. Hermit told me that he watched this shiny maroon Packard drive into his yard, but the shine was hidden by mud that was all over the black fenders and the running boards from all those muddy roads out there. When Hermit asked him who he was and what he wanted, that city slicker announced that he was Bert Benefiel from out of Colorado Springs. He then said that his daughter was planning on marrying one of the local ranchers, a Mr. Gene Johnson. Hermit told me that's when he got mad and flat out refused to answer any questions this big shot was trying to ask him, so the man just drove away."

At this point, Gene turned his head to spit onto the ground beside the bench. Marjora had hoped that this signaled the end of this craziness, but his anger was still raging. In fact, he had totally lost his temper.

He then told her that Hermit had finally remembered where he'd heard the name of Benefiel before, that it had been connected to that 10-year-old murder on Christmas Day up in Manitou.

Now in a totally uncontrolled rage, Gene yelled out,

"Your daddy is a cop!"

7

The wedding *did* take place. The traveling Reverend John Jordan pronounced them man and wife on June 21, 1933, in Colorado Springs at the Benefiel's home on Cheyenne Boulevard. Some of Marjora's friends attended, with Minnie Stafford serving as the bride's Maid of Honor. All of Gene's family attended except for Mark who resided in Vermont. His brother Poole stood up for him as his best man.

The black and white photograph of all the assembled guests taken outside on the front lawn turned out to be tremendously revealing, a testament to the deep feelings that Mr. Bert Blair Benefiel had for his new son-in-law, the man who had snatched his daughter away. Every person in the grouping is looking right at the camera with the exception of Bert. Instead, his head is turned toward the center from his position on the left flank, with a look, a hard look of absolute disdain if not pure hatred focused right on the groom who took up the front and center next to Marjora in her gorgeous white wedding dress of satin accented with delicate lace.

After 3 full days and nights of honeymooning up in Denver, a location the couple referred to as Northern Colorado, they drove in the old Model A out to the country and the little house just outside of Peyton to start their ranch life together.

By the end of just 1 entire week of that life, Marjora was thoroughly disgusted.

Oh, without any question, she had been completely infatuated with the blue-eyed rancher who had so thoroughly swept her off her feet during that concert in Colorado Springs just under a year earlier, and she still felt that she really did love him even after his despicable behavior during their talk in May when he had completely blown up and said all those terrible things about her father. She had yielded to his plea to just "bury the hatchet" during the drive back to her home that same day and had chosen to forgive him but knew in her heart that she would never be able to forget it; she did not intend to try, either. Her father was her hero. He always had been and would continue to be just that. He had so much class and sophistication as he carried out the role of a true gentleman—something that Marjora realized Gene would never be capable of. What had she gotten herself into, she worried?

There was so much indignity in the chores that had befallen her out on the ranch, and Marjora seemed unable to cope with some of them. Without running water, she was reduced to drawing water from the well outside by the chicken coop where she had to gather eggs from the 20 hens that nested there. But by far the worst insult was the trip out to the nasty pig pen to throw potato skins and other slop for the filthy animals to eat, a place that literally made her gag from the foul odor. It really infuriated her that the stench seemingly lingered in her nose all day long after the morning walk out to the pen.

And how was she supposed to keep the house clean with those nasty dust storms blowing through every day? Inside, the house would be sweltering from the summer heat with no open window for ventilation since dirt was swirling everywhere outside. Marjora hated wind. She had very often felt afraid during childhood, especially at night, when winds blew. She had even informed Gene in a letter last winter that wind frightened her. Little did she know that it would be non-stop out on the barren plains.

Each sister-in-law, Helen, Rhoda, and Genevieve had tried to encourage her by offering sweet assurances that she would eventually adjust to the country way of living. Suggestions were given for mixing up the menu somewhat, to use fresh pork and fresh poultry from off the ranch a bit more often. She was told that serving biscuits one supper then cornbread the next day would help break up the monotony of all those usual meals of pinto beans and potatoes.

Marjora would manage to have supper on the table each evening by the time Gene came in from a day spent hoeing the weeds that were trying to overtake the cornfield. His arrival at the wash station out by the well would always be announced by singing. But what was the tune, exactly? It was simply, "Tra la la" repeated over and over again to what was probably "Mockingbird Hill." She wished instead that he would come inside singing his favorite song from last spring while they were still dating, that beautiful song from Bing Crosby called, "Just an Echo in the Valley." But Marjora wouldn't learn until later that this special song really wasn't about them at all, but about the only true love Gene ever had, a woman from Ohio who had ditched him on their wedding day.

She had completed an entire summer of misery out in the country and was now pregnant. Her days were most often spent lying in bed from what was turning out to be an extremely difficult pregnancy. Now the corn harvest was underway in mid-September with Gene coming in after an exhausting day only to find her feeling sickly without a satisfactory explanation for why the house was in such disarray with the bed unmade and supper biscuits on the table that were often burned on the bottoms and already cold.

She feared what her best friend, Lois Armet, would think of her these days in her current predicament. Lois seemed to have married well and was now living up in Denver with her husband, Leon, who practiced anesthesiology at Denver General Hospital. Letters had been exchanged between them, but Marjora left out the absolute drudgery of her day-to-day life.

Another letter had also been written and mailed to her parent's address up at 312 Cheyenne Boulevard in Colorado Springs. In it Marjora had expressed her desperate desire to return home because she could not take any more of the hideous life out in "these sticks." She felt fairly certain that her parents would readibly oblige her and drive out to take her back to the Springs, so she provided detailed timing for the upcoming Thursday, saying that Gene would be out on the far west side of the cornfield from probably about 6 to at least 3 or even later that afternoon and would not be able to see the house at all. Even the long driveway and the road would not be visible. The plan would be to gather up her necessary things and then leave a note of farewell on the kitchen table.

The sight of her daddy's maroon Packard pulling up to the house made her heart leap. She just knew he would come through! She had already written the note of goodbye and hurriedly placed it over on the little table, then grabbed her 2 bags and stepped out onto the porch and beamed at her parents who had not yet emerged from the sedan. Her father jumped out to quickly open the back door for her, acting in a rushed manner while furtively scanning the cornfield hoping to not see Gene walking up toward the house.

The vehicle moved slowly along the dirt road to avoid making a cloud of dust as they headed out toward Highway 24, the escape route back to her parents and their civilized home and lifestyle. Suddenly that same old nausea that had so relentlessly plagued her during the last 2 months returned. She squeezed her eyes shut to avoid being disturbed by any motion outside the windows. But just as quickly as the wave arrived it dissipated, and she was able to finally speak from the back seat.

"Daddy, momma, thank you! Thanks for coming to get me! I really couldn't take any more of that place. I couldn't take any more of that man, either."

There was not an immediate response from either of them. The pause seemed to drag on and on until the silence was finally shattered by Bert's extremely loud and scolding voice,

"I *told* you not to marry that totally worthless, good-for-nothing pig farmer!"

Marjora and her mother began to cry ever so softly. She braced herself for anything further that the man might say in anger, but there was nothing more. Bert had already said what he felt needed to be said, and that was that. He allowed the chips to fall wherever they were meant to fall.

When they drove onto the blacktop, Hope spoke and steered a new conversation that would include their daughter in the information that Bert had managed to collect on her new husband. As the story unfolded, Marjora at first felt betrayed not only by Gene but also by her parents, but it didn't take long to fully understand that they had simply followed reasoned advice from her father who had thought it best not to ruin their marriage from the very outset by telling her everything he knew—and never really wanted to know—about this broken-down man who had only taken Marjora while on the rebound from a woman named Millie that just about everyone out in the country said he was not over. No, not over her at all.

Marjora's emotions then swung toward sympathy for Gene over the terrible loss he had suffered, a loss not only of his fiancé but his ranch as well. But that sympathy did not run very deep and soon vanished all together as she thought back on the 3 months she had managed to remain with that man. Now she understood why he had so often called her "Matilda" with a laugh in his voice. How dare he just use her as his second fiddle!

And now, carrying his unborn child back to the city, she found herself liking the thought that he was, at least in some twisted sort of way, being jilted all over again. And to Marjora's way of thinking, her husband was getting exactly what he deserved.

As the car reached the outskirts of the town, Bert started to change the discussion to only small talk, mostly about the congestion on the roadway with so many people driving about on this Thursday. He then pulled the car to a stop in front of Mabel's Side-Walk Sundaes and inquired of the ladies' what flavors he could bring out to them. This quite refreshing way of bringing what had been a difficult conversation to an end brought a smile to everyone as they sat in the big Packard and enjoyed their waffle cones overflowing with French vanilla ice cream.

Yes. Life was good yet again!

The small brown train case opens to reveal a treasure trove of letters with 3-cent stamps still attached and endless black and white photographs from the early 20th century. Almost all of these glossy pictures have names and dates handwritten on them, some found on the back but often on the front borders, mostly along the bottom but sometimes continuing up the sides in a very real nod to posterity.

Family members and friends from every subsequent generation pouring over these items catch whiffs of sheer antiquity within the weathered case, scents of the yellowing paper and the dried ink. They scarcely recognize any of the figures in the photographs but may recall having heard some of the names that are written. Girls and ladies with odd names like Eleanor or Ethel or Lois or Opal may ring with familiarity. The menfolk from that era yield names like Clifford and Fred mixed in with Melvin and Poole before a Wilbur shows up to complete the pose.

Great grandchildren viewing the contents of the case marvel at the names that are completely unlike their own. They all insist that their personal names could never sound strange or outdated like these do.

But there the relatives all stand in the photographs, appearing totally unashamed, as if everyone's name is completely normal.

All are dressed in their Sunday best with mostly hard stares toward the camera, often with a squint against the bright Colorado sunshine. And all, whether fully grasping it or not, are forevermore captured for their lives to be viewed and pondered by those who will follow.

WHILE YOU HAVE THE CHANCE

1

The farmhouse roof and most of the 2nd story were already fully engulfed in roaring, hissing flames, but she had somehow managed to grab the still-sleeping baby from his crib just as a far corner of the bedroom ceiling came crashing down, dropping burning debris that skidded across the floor in her direction. She screamed in terror and almost fell as she jumped out of the way. Her grasp on the 1-month-old was still firm, but his little blanket kept trying to slip out of her hands. And by now the infant was wailing at a volume that matched her continued screaming.

Only a young 1st grader herself, the sister knew that it was completely up to her to save them both from perishing. She was panicking, yes, but she knew she had to get them out of the burning house. It had to be now!

The smoke was very dense and blocking her view, but she remembered that just across from the bedroom door would be the set of stairs that she had dashed up moments earlier. She told herself not to stumble on a single step if she ever hoped to rejoin the other family members who were still in their nightclothes huddled in the snow-covered front yard, shivering, and crying and yelling for her to hurry.

Then suddenly the little girl burst out onto the front porch, sobbing hysterically but still holding her baby brother, the newest member of this Illinois family. He was only in his pajamas with no blanket wrapped around him, but she had succeeded in rescuing him from the burning house in which he had been born only days earlier in the old and weathered clapboard farmhouse sitting up near the road 3 miles south of Rockford. Now that birthplace would very soon be nothing but a pile of ashes as it burned to the ground.

"Oh, Ellen!" her mother called out, "You got Kenny! You got my baby!"

Tears streamed down her face as she ran up to grab them both. All the others then crowded around in a crushing hug of gratitude as the father exclaimed,

"Everybody got out! Everyone's out! We're all safe!"

The family quickly ran further out into the snow-filled yard as the entire 2nd story suddenly plunged down into the center of the burning house, sending flames and orange sparks soaring high up into the overcast morning sky. Everyone's face was horror-stricken as the family watched the only home they had known vaporize before their eyes.

2

Times were hard. Very hard. Every farmer around the Monroe Center area knew he was ruined when crop prices dropped by more than 50% while the Great Depression swept over the country. But what they didn't know was that the total economic destruction would last all through the 1930s and be followed by the Second World War that would take so many men away from the farms to be sent off to fight in foreign lands. And no farmer could have ever foreseen the rationing of food and other basic goods that was yet to come.

Practically every farming family would gather around the transistor radio right after supper to listen to the evening news, when Gabriel Heatter would always begin every broadcast with the words, "There's good news tonight!" But where was the good news for all of them, exactly? How would the farmers manage to afford that necessary part to get the tractor running again in order to turn the fields and plant the corn or soybeans or the wheat? Where would the cash come from to even buy the seed?

Many folks had no choice but to give up. Too many foreclosures and forced auctions of their acreage, animals, farm equipment and household furnishings had completely discouraged them. If not their own, they certainly knew a few families that had lost their farm and almost everything that had been their life. And everyone had heard the disturbing news that the topsoil out on the High Plains was just blowing away in what had been labeled the Oklahoma Dust Bowl. Families were pulling up stakes and heading west on Route 66, the "Mother Road," in old vehicles loaded down and piled high with all their worldly belongings, hoping to at least find summer work picking peaches in California or maybe following the cherry harvest up in the Pacific Northwest.

Not every struggling family had decided to go set up housekeeping somewhere else further west, though. The lucky ones had nearby kin that they could rely on for advice and sometimes for small amounts of cash that helped tide them over for a spell.

Such was the situation with Oscar and Rose Ella Hill. The chimney fire that had burned their farmhouse to the ground had forced them into town, to that small apartment down on Sixth Avenue where everyone crowded into the cramped quarters until something else became available, something bigger that would better house a family with 9 children. The oldest son, Bill, one of the twins, was away working on Jim Blair's farm, earning his room and board there by handling the milk cows. At least only 8 children were crammed into the small apartment.

The trauma from the loss of housing for his family had hit Oscar rather hard. Still, he was very grateful that Nathan Caruthers, the apartment manager, had understood his desperate need and allowed them all to move in.

He had known real trauma before, the kind that had come while on the frontlines fighting in the trenches of Germany during the First World War. But he had managed to endure that terror rather well without any outward signs of what was commonly referred to as shell shock; he was determined to withstand this current housing loss just as well.

Long after returning home from overseas when the war had ended, government checks generated by the Bonus Act for at least $1000, with some coming in as high as $1600, finally arrived in the mailbox of every surviving veteran. What a godsend that turned out to be for Mr. Oscar Hill, who immediately purchased a 3-story house on Fourth Avenue that was finally big enough for his entire family to live in comfortably. It was across the street from White Swan Elementary and Abraham Lincoln Junior High Schools, making the location perfect for all his children who would play on the swing sets and merry-go-rounds, the baseball diamond and basketball courts, and the open fields for soccer and football. Could it have been any better than this?

By the time Kenny had grown from the rescued infant way out at that burning farmhouse to his 1st year in junior high across the street at Lincoln, his parent's marriage had already basically fallen apart. Neither parent was entirely to blame for the disintegration of their vows that were totally dissolved by 1940.

Since they no longer farmed, both had jobs in town, with Oscar Hill working the evening shift at Garrison's machine shop just west of Rockford's manufacturing district where his primary duty was to maintain the equipment in smooth running order. Rose spent her workdays out at the furniture manufacturing plant on the edge of the town, but eventually accepted higher-paying work at the Camp Grant Army facility.

It was inevitable, actually. Ken's father couldn't even leave the shop until exactly 11:30 every night, and his mother returned home every evening around 6 or so, but it got to be later and later until one evening she failed to return at all. The divorce judge granted full custody of the youngest children who were still living at home to Oscar, and it wasn't until almost a year later that every family member finally heard about a marriage between an Army sergeant and the mother of too many children who had chosen to finally move on with her life.

"Would you like to buy some ice cream? I've only got 3 flavors, but they're all really good!"

Ken was now a teenager with his own real job driving the company truck around to the area farms hawking just about everyone's favorite summertime treat. Of course, the profit margin was extremely slim indeed, but he still managed to squeeze out a little bit for himself from time to time. And besides, he was very busy honing his craft as a salesman, the profession that would come to define his entire adult career.

His vehicle was a used 4-door Model A Roadster that cost his dad and older brother exactly $10 from funds they had managed to cobble together. And that Ford turned out to be reliable transportation, taking him up to college at the University of Wisconsin for just a single semester of pre-pharmacy study and then over to the little town of Tomahawk where he worked at Mossman Brothers learning the pharmacy business. He fully intended to return to his college studies, of course, when he could save enough for his tuition, fees, and room and board. The plan was to work a semester alternating with a semester at school to get the degree he would need. But he had to pay his own way, since his dad only earned exactly 34 cents every hour at his job and simply had no funds to spare for paying for any college expenses.

But as it turned out, Uncle Sam had entirely different plans for Kenneth Hill and every other able-bodied man from everywhere around. The ferocious winds of war were already blowing very hard on the Korean Peninsula and there was an acute need for additional men to go fight in that foreign war. So, that dreaded "Greeting. You are hereby ordered to report" draft notice had almost immediately caught up with him.

There was never any question whatsoever about the branch of service he would end up volunteering for. His much-older brother Bill, who Kenneth had always idolized, had served in the Navy, first as an enlisted man and then in the officer ranks as the Executive Officer for an amphibious LST landing craft that went ashore on Iwo Jima for that 5-week battle during the Second World War.

No, there was no question! Ken would walk into the Naval Recruiting Office to sign up for his tour of duty!

Since the Navy had no training available for enlisted sailors who desired to learn the pharmacy business short of becoming an actual pharmacist, Ken chose instead to train to be an operating room technician, with surgery being an ideal place to work while he put in the time that the Navy had demanded of him.

5

"Hey, Dave, have you seen that charge nurse over on the ward, the pretty little blond one? That's my gal, all right. I will be marrying that girl before any of us ship out. You'll see!"

She was not the typical Navy nurse at all. Petite and gorgeous, she continuously carried herself with the authority expected of a Naval officer, yet there did seem to be that flirtatious side to her—at least when Ken was around, anyway. Hadn't she ever-so-slightly smiled back at him as he passed by her last week with that large double pack of linen? And when his path deliberately crossed hers yet again with another pack some 15 minutes later, hadn't she lingered just long enough for him to brush up against her left hand as she returned those patient charts to the rack? His heart raced as it fully registered with him that it had happened just that way!

Everyone knew there could be no fraternity between the enlisted and officer ranks, yet he felt magnetized to her, using every possible excuse he could think of to go over to the adjacent building where the Junior Grade Lieutenant managed the nurses who took care of those lined up in the hospital beds on the ward.

There was a thrill to this chase. It was the kind of risk that always kept the blood churning while requiring an active look around to not get busted outright. But the real danger, however, came from his friends who might not be discrete enough to stay quiet, especially that clown Reginald Smith from Massachusetts who considered practically everything, even life itself, to be nothing more than a joke. But Ken knew he could trust his closest friend, Dave, and his secret courtship was probably safe with the others who knew about it, like Stephenson and even Dr. Reed. But this trust had to hold. It absolutely had to.

Her name was Mary, and she came from Southport, North Carolina. Ken had never heard anyone speak with that curious Southern accent, and he absolutely loved it. Nobody had ever talked like that up in the Midwest, that was very certain. And never had a girl tugged at him the way she seemed to, a tugging that was ever-so-gentle without any pushiness or even a trace of judgement of his Midwestern values or his humble upbringing.

Ken and Mary's clandestine courtship was much like a whirlwind. It was true that Ken would be shipping out very soon; transfer orders had already been cut for somewhere out in California, so there was simply no time left to squander. A plan had to be forged now and executed before he got sent over to Korea where just about every man was headed.

And finally, "By the authority vested in me by the Commonwealth of Virginia, I hereby pronounce you man and wife."

The honeymoon of Mr. and Mrs. Ken Hill took place in Newport News, Virginia and was comprised solely of the 2 days of Ken's leave that remained before his deployment out to the Pacific theatre. But his trusted old companion, a Studebaker convertible, helped to make those few days very sweet indeed.

Mary had visited the Chief Nurse for the Naval Base to state that she intended to immediately surrender her Naval officer's commission to marry the enlisted sailor, Kenneth Eugene Hill. Not surprisingly, Mary's reception was extremely cold. The stern, unmarried female Chief was certain that she had completely lost her mind to be giving up such a promising career in the U.S. Navy Nurse Corps to even get married in the first place, let alone to someone who wasn't even an officer. And she said as much. Mary's reply was truly smooth, fit for the cinema. She very calmly said,

"You know, real, true love never circles around a 2nd time, so you'd be wise to batten it down while you have the chance!"

Hospitalman Second Class Hill never actually set foot on any Korean soil at all. Initially stationed in Japan, good luck and shrewd maneuvering kept him there throughout his entire enlistment in the Navy. Every time a promotion and exam came up, Kenneth would secure a 30-day leave. Complicit in this scheme was his superior, Russel Sexton out of Colorado, who had become his friend and removed his name from every transport manifest, using not only leave tactics but also transferring him over to the linen room on one occasion to escape the war.

The real motivation for blocking the transfer of Hill, though, was very simple. He was the shortstop for a military baseball team in Japan, the Navy team that remained undefeated for the nearly 3 years that Ken played shortstop on the team. He was irreplaceable in that position, and he was fully credited with that spectacular homerun hit with the ball sailing way out over the fence! Who else could do that?

By the time he had finished his tour in the Navy and was a civilian again, his return to Illinois was marked by being a family man. His daughter, Susan, had just turned 18 months old when he was finally home to stay, and she looked at him as if to say,

"Who's he, Mommy?"

In desperate need of employment to support his wife and toddler, he gathered them into his 1950 DeSoto and traveled 2000 miles from Illinois out to California to interview with the State Farm Insurance manager, John McCloud. He was advised to immediately take the casualty, life and health examinations required to obtain state licensure in California. By September, his passing results arrived in the morning mail, and the appropriate advice and gracious direction given by Mr. John McCloud would forever be remembered as Kenneth Hill's highly successful State Farm Insurance career in California began.

From the early days of door-to-door ice cream sales as a young teenager in Illinois to selling and servicing insurance policies out in California until retirement at the age of 57, his salesmanship abilities were always on full display. From sales to training director, then from an agency in Bakersfield to the coveted one that he managed to acquire over on the coast in Ventura, his family greatly benefitted from what had always seemed to everyone to be his effortless one-on-one business talent and capability.

Along the way, while living down in Orange County, his family soon expanded with the birth of his 2 sons, Kenneth, Jr., and Craig. Both boys, like their father, were quite athletic and played on their respective high school football teams, with Ken positioned as a linebacker that few opponents ever really got past and Craig as the kicker with precision shots through the uprights.

And Susan followed in her own mother's footsteps by becoming a licensed Registered Nurse and working in Intensive Care Units for years before finally retiring as an Infection Preventionist.

8

It did not require a microscope focused directly on the marriage of Ken and Mary Hill to clearly see that it was one that was marked by a genuine love for one another. That very same initial spark that they both felt while stationed together at Chicago's Great Lakes Naval Base continued throughout all their 50 years as a married couple. But could it really be that Mary's famed North Carolina cookery played an enormous part in the success of the marriage? After all, if a wife can't cook, what's a man to do, anyway?

But it was so much more than that. They had both determined, right from the start of their marriage, to consistently treat each other with open respect and genuine kindness. That proved, overall, to be their winning combination!

And neither of them had ever forgotten the absolute truth found in the statement that Mary had so boldly proclaimed on that day when she gave up her Naval Officers Commission for Ken:

"You know, real, true love never circles around a 2nd time, so you'd be wise to batten it down while you have the chance!"

TROUBLE FROM THE THIRD ROW

1

Never had I been to any school before, and the whole thing terrified me. And never had any bigger, blacker, meaner dog ever chased me like this. I was much too scared to keep walking on that dirt road, the one that headed north from our house down on the corner of McGaffey Street up to the elementary school. Even though I was accompanied by both my older brother and sister who would be attending the same school on this 1st day of the school year, this 6-year-old boy heading to school was simply unable to cope with the menace behind that chain link fence.

The plan for getting up to the school before the bell sounded was so simple. It only required walking past that house with that aggressive yard dog. My sister, Gladys, knew this and did her very best to convince me that I was not in any real danger. After all, we had already heard the furious barking long before we reached the fenced yard, since our brother David had run way on ahead of us and had not been attacked. Absolutely certain that the huge black monster was reserving the actual biting only for me, I continued on toward the yard while desperately clinging to my sister's skirt. Even before we got to the house beside the road, I was already bawling and refused to take another step.

"Johnny, stop that crying! Just stop it! That dog is *inside* the fence. Now just come on. We have to go this way to get to school."

And then she pulled me into a run. At least we were running! But that snarling dog headed to the corner of the yard and started running right along beside us, running so fast and barking so loudly that I just knew I would be bitten within seconds.

2

After safely arriving at the schoolhouse with no dog bites, my sister walked with me into the class where the middle-aged teacher, Mrs. Devlin, welcomed me with a bright smile before searching for my name on her seating chart. I then watched in agony as Gladys departed the classroom, leaving me alone with the teacher, my desk, and all the other 1st graders.

His name was Gregory and he sat at an end desk just 1 row behind me but across the aisle to my left. Red-headed with freckles covering his face, he appeared clownish with a ready smile and bright red sneakers with white shoelaces to complete the look.

It all happened immediately after the lunch period. Each pupil had been instructed by Mrs. Devlin to lay his head on the desktop with eyes closed for a short period of rest. The whole exercise seemed rather silly to me, and I really struggled to comply. Twisting my head over to my left side, I spotted Gregory who was looking over toward me with a huge grin on his face. And then he did it! He stuck out his tongue and made that obscene sound that caused his tongue and his lower lip to flutter. Many students turned around to peek at the offender, but I, with direct eye contact, started giggling and just couldn't stop. Gregory was laughing, too, and rather loudly.

Mrs. Devlin quickly rose from her desk at the front of the classroom. Every student heard her sturdy, thick-heeled shoes as they clattered across the hardwood floor. She made a beeline straight to me where I was sitting in the 2nd row and stopped to verify that I was the culprit who was loudly giggling non-stop. Then she whirled around to discover Gregory doing the same.

What followed next really caught me by surprise. The teacher demanded that Gregory stand up and lean forward across the back of his chair. Dangling from her right hand was a huge wooden paddle which she used to smack on his backside exactly 3 times. And after that whipping, she turned to me and said,

"Young man, stand up and lean over your chair!"

Three whacks later I sat down, still laughing but in a much more controlled manner. I made eye contact with Gregory once again. He was still quietly giggling.

This newfound friend and I hung out together during the next recess, with a group of other boys gathered around to help us celebrate the 2 spankings—and on the very 1st day of school, at that!

3

By the last day of the 2nd week of our journey to and from school on the road that passed that monstrous dog, he had apparently just grown tired of the chase. Three young schoolchildren were no longer of much interest to him anymore, since he would now prefer to continue his napping rather than regard us as any real menace to himself or to the house he protected.

But all 3 of us continued to walk way over on the far side of the road as we passed that yard. After all, we could never be too careful.

RAINY DAY PAINT JOB

There had been a pressing question hovering around the place for several days, something that just kept lingering as each weekday slowly passed. "When will this blasted rain ever stop?" It was October, and cold, but this much rain seemed unusual.

There were no standing puddles of rainwater outside like after the August cloudbursts, those late summer monsoon storms that generally started with a dust storm but finally yielded to a real gully washer that was always so welcome. These desert storms cooled down the heat, a relentless 100-degree heat, a heat that could actually be seen rising in waves from the desert floor off in the distance when looking north from the bedroom window. There were many folks, both old-timers and young alike, who swore that if you stared at those heat waves long enough, day after endless day from inside a sweltering house, you would start to believe that you were slowing going crazy.

This was definitely not that kind of rain, but instead a slow and soaking one, the kind of wet weather that usually made you feel the cold right down into your bones. The rain had started sometime before dawn on Sunday, and it really needed to stop. There were big plans afoot for Saturday!

The announcement had been made at the kitchen table on that Monday morning as I hurriedly wolfed down the never-changing breakfast of a single fried egg with exactly 2 cracker squares. My parents had finished their meal a whole hour earlier but were still seated around the table, as always, drinking cup after cup of boiled coffee from the pot that was always kept hot on the stovetop nearby.

Suddenly, without warning, Daddy broke the normal silence of the morning breakfast time. Not stating my name but looking straight at me, he said,

"We'll be heading into town on Saturday to find you a car if it ever stops raining. You should never buy a car when it rains. You know that, don't you? You just can't tell what the paint job looks like if it's wet."

I must have mumbled something about bad paint jobs and wet cars since I remember choking on the dry cracker in my mouth. Because I was so red-faced and had no idea what to say to my dad anyway, I stood to leave the table, snatching up my books and calling out to my 2 sisters to hurry up or we'd miss the bus.

Filing past the end of the kitchen table to leave by the back door, we performed the Monday morning ritual of pocketing 1 of the dollar bills laid out in a row that represented our meager weekly allowance. We could feel their searching, even piercing, eyes, especially our mother's, watching every move as we touched that money. The entire process was mortifying to us, but we still somehow managed to squeak out a soft "thank you" in the general direction of where they were both seated before stepping out into the rain falling on the unpainted wooden porch.

What? How could this be? I was really going to have a car in high school. At 17, the peach fuzz on my face had just become acquainted with razors and Styptic pencils, and now I would have my very own car. A man with a car. Unbelievable!

Incredibly good fortune had definitely come my way; my 2 older sisters had not been given a car at all, and my older brother had to wait until the end of summer just before he headed off to the university on the full-ride scholarship he had earned to get his $100 Ford sedan. Now it was my turn—and a year early!

Did I skip along the muddy trail up to the corner bus stop, both from pure delight and to outrun the rain? Probably. Yes, the rain was still falling, but who really cared today? Both of my sisters were as giddy with excitement as I was. It was cold and we were getting soaked, but we hadn't noticed until the bus arrived. We then climbed onboard, shivering from the cold with our clothes sopping wet.

We were happy that wet October morning in 1965. It didn't matter so much on that Monday that we were just 3 very poor kids from that shack behind us. And at least our shabby house wasn't over there, over on the other side of the blacktop road, over there in what everybody had always called Dogtown. At least there was that!

"Nah, I don't have anything for just $100 bucks," the elderly salesman replied. "Nothing at that price for a year or probably even 2 now, at least. But don't you start worrying. I'll show you what I've got right back over there."

We followed him to the rear of his car lot to 2 short line-ups of much older cars, several with faded paint and some with dents and old scars that spoke of their long and abused history.

"Right over there. That big one. See that beauty? Two hundred dollars cash and you can drive it right off the lot today, young man. She's ready, and there's a full tank of gas in her, to boot!"

Backed into the last row and looking right back at me with those near-dual headlights was a long, low, and enormously wide 1957 Plymouth Savoy sedan in an off-white color with 4 doors and large tail fins. And I was sure that I'd caught the left headlight flicker for a second as if to say that she was meant to be my car, my very own personal treasure, if I could just come up with that extra $100.

Daddy always carried his cash money, both bills and coins, in the front pocket of his baggy brown slacks in that small leather pocketbook with the shiny metal clasp on top. Holding my breath as he unfolded each $20 bill, I watched as he ever so slowly passed them over to the salesman. Had there been enough folded bills in that little brown purse, or would he be forced to bargain for a lesser price for my perfect car sitting right over there?

My breathless excitement must have been obvious to that car salesman, since he knew it was to be my very first car. As he watched us, he was undoubtedly reminded of the many other times he had witnessed similar interactions between a father and son on his used car lot down on South Main Street.

But this Saturday morning walk-on just might have seemed somewhat different. With no other buyers anywhere around, we would have had his undivided attention. He would have noticed the awkwardness in the relationship between the youth and his 70-year-old father as we all milled around the vehicle. Maybe he would have even seen the furtive glances I had made over to my father when he kicked the left rear tire, then walked around to kick at the one on the other side, too. Maybe he even noticed the look of absolute relief on my face when that old practice borne out of the Great Depression hadn't continued to the front tires!

When the man got into the drivers' seat and started the car for us, my heart leaped at the first sound of that mighty V8 engine as it came alive! It seemed to roar when he pressed the accelerator, and my heart roared right along with it. But my dad wasn't really impressed with that beautiful gas-guzzling music. No. He had slipped around to the back end of the car and was earnestly studying the exhaust pipe, determined to detect any tale-tale sign of that bluish smoke that would reveal a tired engine needing new rings and whatever else. Knowing that a deal killer was possibly in the making, I also went around to the back to see any evidence for myself. To my great relief, only the slightest wisps of light gray condensation greeted the cold morning air.

After the paperwork for the Title and Bill of Sale was completed, I slid into the seat behind that massive steering wheel while the powerful engine sang in my ears. But it wasn't very long before that old saying about never being able to trust a used car salesman hit me squarely between the eyes. The needle on the fuel gauge was practically sitting right on empty!

It seemed that Daddy must have known something about these salesmen, too. When he leaned his head through the open window to search the dash for the fuel gauge, I could smell the strong, black coffee on his breath. When I pointed to the evidence of the near-empty tank, he clicked his tongue and withdrew his head and began fishing around in his pants pocket again. Pulling out a crumpled $5 bill, he said,

"This should fill that tank right up. You go on ahead and fill up with gasoline and then head on home—or wherever you're going. I've still got a few things to do here in town."

For just a fleeting moment our eyes locked together, and I was certain that I detected a slight twinkle in his eyes just before he turned away.

4

Driving west toward Six Mile Hill with a tank full of leaded gas and pop music from the local AM station, KBIM, playing on the car radio, I rehearsed the events of this wonderful Saturday. The late October sun was shining directly overhead onto the roadway that was dry since that dreadful rain had just up and vanished away the previous afternoon. My huge, powerful car was carrying me along on the smoothest ride I had ever experienced.

Without any doubt, though, my dad had spent pretty much every bit of the money he had for my car, and that awareness did cause me some real nervousness. But it wasn't enough to dampen my joy. After all, he had willingly spent it on his son who needed a car. That truth would stay with me forever.

And just for the record, the paint job on my sweet, sweet Plymouth was perfect, whether the day was wet or dry!

MOMMA'S CHEVROLET

The rolling dust cloud announced the arrival of the car before we even heard the tires on the bumpy dirt track that ran down toward the house from up at the corner of Brown Road. When the choking dust blew on ahead of the vehicle while it rolled to a stop, what remained was an unsightly wreck of a sedan in some ghastly color only found at one of those inexpensive Earl Scheib paint and body shops.

We quickly slid down from our perches on the butane tank and crowded around to get an up-close look at the sedan. Even Shadrach trotted over to investigate, letting out short, excited barks of welcome.

The girls wouldn't know the year or model of the car, but I instantly saw that it was a Chevrolet, a 1954 Bel Air sedan with 4 doors and white-wall tires with full chrome hubcaps and push button door handles.

The back bumper had rust running along the entire bottom, and a long scrape about 4 inches wide ran across the right rear door that had only been painted over. The chrome bumper in front was missing the bumper guard on the driver's side, giving the grill a lopsided appearance. While all the window glass was intact, a corner-to-corner crack had traveled across the windshield.

And just what color was the paint, anyway? Was it supposed to be pink? The car was a 2-tone from the factory, with the roof in faded eggshell white. But the car body was painted in a very unusual shade of pink. Pink!

Suddenly both front doors squeaked open and out climbed our parents. Daddy wore his familiar smirk as he averted our gaze, as always, but Momma wore an enormous smile as she looked around at all of us, a smile that seemed to say, "Just look at this!"

Quickly jumping into the now-available front seat, I began to investigate the inside of the car. The floors were covered with plush, fitted carpet, and the dash had a working clock in it, both firsts for this Johnson family. And the transmission was automatic, believe it or not, yet another first! An overhead dome light completed the interior.

Boy, had we ever moved up in this world!

2

They had boarded the 5:10 PM Greyhound bus out to Phoenix on a Thursday in early March for the nearly 10-hour ride through the night with rest stops in Las Cruces and Lordsburg before the final stop in Globe, Arizona. By the time they got to the bus station on east Van Buren Street, the morning sky was already beginning to signal that dawn was fast approaching. All the snacks that Momma had packed were already long gone and they were hungry for a good breakfast and desperate for a cup of coffee. Splurging a little on a taxicab to carry them to Stan's Cabins, the cabin camp where they had stayed several times before, they checked in and then immediately walked to the little all-night café across the street.

After their breakfast of scrambled eggs with sausage and pancakes, they sipped their mugs of hot coffee and made their plans for the day. Since the whole purpose of the trip out to Phoenix was to pick up an inexpensive car to drive back over to New Mexico to use as a trade-in for another used Chevrolet pickup, the morning would be spent walking up Van Buren past the many used car lots that lined both sides of this wide city street. But Daddy already knew that the lots with the vehicles that he might be able to afford were generally only on the north side of the street traveling west from their lodging place. It was in that direction that they headed out.

The budget for securing a car to drive back to Roswell was $200, hopefully less. Even in 1965 dollars, that was probably not enough money for a used car that anyone would really want to be caught dead in, let alone one that could properly define a person while driving through his own hometown.

As it turned out, luck was on their side. Within only an hour of walking past the lots, a cheap sedan was found. The vehicle was priced at just $225, and it was even a Chevrolet! How could that be any better?

After they had driven the car around for a few blocks and found that it ran well, Daddy bargained the price down by $25 and they drove away, happy that they still had all their grocery money left and that they actually had a vehicle to drive during the week-long vacation that the trip to Arizona now represented.

A drive down to the Bashas' Supermarket to stock up on food supplies for the week was necessary. Almost everything that was placed into the grocery shopping cart would not require refrigeration. Even the little can of Carnation evaporated milk used for Momma's morning coffee would stay out on the kitchenette's counter, as would the oleo, longhorn cheese, and the ripening cantaloupe. The bottles of Sprite soda pop, though, and the big watermelon would take up what little space could be found in the small Frigidaire in the room. But the best thing was that the appliance would have a small freezer section at the very top for 2 metal ice cube trays plus a half-gallon of Neapolitan ice cream!

And no trip to a grocery store was ever fully complete before making a swing by the fresh bakery section in hopes of finding day-old donuts packaged for sale.

The return to Roswell in Momma's favorite Chevrolet occurred on a Tuesday a week later, and it didn't take more than a single day for Daddy to start tearing the deal completely apart.

First of all, it had power steering. And wasn't it the steering fluid reservoir that was leaking much like a sieve onto the ground underneath the car even now? And second, the vehicle had that blasted automatic transmission. Since he always handled all automotive repairs himself, he was pretty worried that his lack of experience with automatics could present a very big problem. All the power steering unit needed was a new rubber gasket, of course, but what about that Powerglide transmission when it started slipping or just decided to freeze up entirely? He knew nothing about a transmission with a torque converter. Where would he start in trying to repair such a complicated part of this Bel Air if it failed?

Momma loved the car and really wanted him to keep it. She had countered his misgivings about the sedan by reminding him that it had performed like a dream while driving around the Phoenix area for the week of vacation. Further, she mentioned that the drive home along the highways had gone very well, with excellent power for climbing up to Globe past those open pit cooper mines without overheating. She also pointed out that the tires were in great condition all around and had given them a smooth ride without a single blowout to slow them down.

Yet she knew exactly how these discussions *always* went.

Her contentment would be limited to a memory, only a memory of that wonderful week in March of 1965 when she had enjoyed feeling positively aristocratic while riding around in her gorgeous pink Chevrolet!

THE GRAND TOUR

Anyone in his right mind would have recognized that the offer was a complete hoax simply because it had to be. Yes, it was officially posted, but nothing about this announcement could possibly be true. Even on the outside chance that it somehow proved to be legitimate, it would have many strings attached, so many that it could never really be acceptable.

But there it was for all to see that Monday morning right at breakfast time, a bulletin from Headquarters Company. It was stapled to the top left corner of the Information Board just outside the entrance to the mess hall at LZ Schueller.

OFFICIAL NOTIFICATION

DATE: Monday, 19 Oct 70
TO: All Clinical Specialist Medical Personnel
SUBJECT: Extension of Commitment
CONTACT: Maj. Scott Taylor
DIVISION: HHC, 1/10 Cavalry, 4th Infantry

The U.S. Army Medical Corps is offering all 91C20 Medics currently stationed in the Republic of Vietnam a one-time opportunity to extend their in-country commitment by six (6) months.

In exchange for this extension, a thirty (30) day leave shall be granted with round-trip airfare by Pan Am Airways to any destination worldwide.

In addition, new duty assignment orders shall be issued for the location of choice anywhere within the entire Vietnam theatre of operations upon return from leave.

Since I was the only medic on the entire compound fitting that occupational specialty, the notice could have come to me alone. Would I have believed the posting more if it had? Probably so. Regardless, there was still something I had to do about this too-good-to-be-true offering.

My good friend Sergeant Major McReynolds was the only person I could trust to analyze this proposal—an offering that had so tightly grabbed onto me. Sarge knew me very well and consistently treated me much more like his son than a junior soldier. I needed his perspective. SGM McReynolds would help me sort this whole thing out.

After waiting until the early afternoon when I felt certain that no one would still be moving around, I sneaked over to the bulletin board and ripped the announcement off, quickly folding the paper and hiding it in my fatigue shirt pocket. Heading over to TOC, the Tactical Operations Center bunker, I located him in his customary spot at the old wooden desk in the corner with his trademark Chesterfield cigarette burning between his yellow-stained fingers. Glancing up, he asked,

"What brings you over in the middle of the day, Doc?"

Opening the folded announcement, I thrust it toward him and exclaimed,

"This!"

He scanned the notice and then immediately handed it back to me.

"I was wondering how long it would take you to see this and want to talk about it."

What? Sarge really did know me that well after all and was many steps ahead of me! He knew that I wanted to work in Saigon at the big Army hospital there and assured me that I would definitely get that assignment since he had already started the transfer paperwork. The question he had was where I wanted to go for a month, but even that was pretty much a given since we had talked so often about Western Europe and my desire to visit all those wonderful countries and peoples. He then informed me that air travel would be covered by military vouchers that would bring me back to Saigon from any location anywhere in the world.

My instructions were clear. The Sergeant Major said I was to have my driver take me to the An Khe Base the following morning to complete paperwork for an expedited passport that would be waiting for pick up when I arrived in Saigon to begin my leave.

Before heading back to LZ Schueller, my driver pulled the Jeep into the Post Exchange parking lot. Inside the store, we searched for desired music on cassette tapes and grabbed special snacks and any reading material that appealed to us. My personal mission was to locate something that would serve as a travel guide for navigating through Europe. To my delight, a guide that I had heard about was displayed along with history books—*Europe on $5 a Day*.

By the time the plane lifted off from Saigon's Tan Son Nhut Airbase for the short flight to Bangkok, I had finally started to relax. The aggravating delay at the upcountry airstrip had not cut into my leave days after all, but it really had been nerve-wracking to be so hopelessly stranded for 2 whole days waiting for a break in the cloud cover from the never-ending rain. The beautiful sound of the C-123 engines could be heard above the clouds a couple of times on the 1st day and once on the 2nd day before the rain stopped and slanting rays of sunshine finally broke through by mid-afternoon. And there it came, diving down out of the clearing skies to the wet runway for my flight down south.

With exactly 30 days to work with, the travel itinerary to Europe had to be carefully planned in detail right down to the final day before I would report to work at the U.S. Army 3rd Field Hospital in Saigon. Hours had been spent doing just that, with only a single day and full night reserved for Thailand on the way out before allotting all of the remaining days to my real destination—Europe!

On the last day of October, the stifling heat and humidity at mid-day in Bangkok were only tolerable when the taxi was moving to allow air flow through the open windows. When an intersection required a stop, my senses were assaulted with blaring horns and choking exhaust from the cars, trucks, scooters, and motorcycles just sitting at idle until the flow of vehicles started forward again. But even that would not interfere with this city tour that I had managed to piece together using very limited travel funds. I was thoroughly immersed in this bustling Asian city, and the next stop, just up ahead on the left, was the Temple of the Golden Buddha.

"It was made from more than 5 tons of solid gold and was constructed 100s of years ago," the young tour guide proclaimed with obvious pride. "This statue is Thailand's most sacred treasure!"

But I had already found a different national treasure at dinner on the previous evening, one that, to this very day, still has me claiming that I must have been Thai in a "previous" life. Otherwise, how else can it be explained?

The elegant plate of jasmine rice surrounded by a semi-circle of colorful dishes like curried chicken and spiced beef, pork broth with thin strands of cabbage, and a large bowl of steamed vegetables along with other exotic delicacies, including a small dessert bowl of sweet sticky rice topped with mango slices, had me at the very first bite!

Pan Am would be covering some 5000 miles between Asia and my first stop in Germany. There would be fuel stops and minor layovers along the way in New Delhi, Tehran, Beirut, and Istanbul, but I would soon bid farewell to any further jet travel in Frankfort and start walking and using taxi cabs and trains for the duration of the tour.

Never having ridden in a Mercedes-Benz taxi before, I was genuinely impressed with the huge interior and smooth and silent ride down to the hotel to begin my European adventure. The room was 3 full flights up the narrow staircase and certainly modest but clean with fresh sheets and a large stack of white towels. And even breakfast was included, beginning at 6 AM. I quickly realized, to my dismay, that these bargain accommodations found in the Frommer guidebook most often would not provide a private bathroom. Instead, all guests were directed to the communal WC down the hallway. Now I was confused. What in this world was a WC? I was way too embarrassed to even ask anyone, so I had to wait until the translation appeared inside another hotel room somewhere else down the line, signage near a dresser topped with towels that spelled out Water Closet.

So, this was breakfast? Exactly 3 extremely thin slices of deli meat along with 2 razor-thin slices of ice-box-cold Pumpernickel bread were arranged on a plate with a small dish of elderberry jam served on the side. A single cup of strong coffee finished off the meal. But hey, at least it was served without charge!

My face remained glued to the left-sided window on the 100-mile train journey down to Stuttgart. As the countryside flashed by, I reflected on the friendship with Captain Harris that we had maintained since those initial training days back in San Antonio. Now stationed in Stuttgart, he had offered to show me around the city where both Porsche and Mercedes-Benz companies were headquartered.

But my interest was in the famed autobahn instead, that legendary free-for-all highway where limits on speed are nothing more than a mere suggestion. And exactly as it has been described time and time again, the approaching car just appeared completely out of nowhere in the rearview mirror of his VW Beetle. The captain alerted me just in time to twist around and see the Mercedes bearing down on us from the fast lane before flashing past and quickly shrinking in size as it continued up the road.

"Whew! How fast was he going, anyway?"

6

The Nord train station in Paris was not only ornate and stately but truly cavernous with a noise level to match. Still in constant use at mid-century, throngs of people made up of businessmen and families and even tourists bustled all around, boarding cars or just transferring to other means of transportation. Even though I wanted to stop momentarily and really soak in the fabulous architecture, the crush of people all around prevented that. Besides, my acting just like a gawking tourist was embarrassing enough, anyway.

It was at the Information window, though, where I caught a first-hand dose of what it meant to be in a foreign country without an ability to speak the native language. I immediately thought of the sensational book published in 1958, *The Ugly American*, that had exposed the absolute disdain for those who expected every single encounter or transaction to be molded strictly into the American way of doing everything. Nevertheless, without any knowledge of the French language, I actually did need someone, anyone who spoke English to help me. But clearly that was not to happen. There I stood in this historic place, a 21-year-old man clutching onto that Samsonite suitcase, not panicking in any way, but left wondering why I felt shunned and even ridiculed for not even knowing the proper language. I sensed that the French were being rude and acting superior to me, and that injured my American pride more than just a little.

Three entire days were spent in Paris, which wasn't nearly enough time. The Louvre Museum alone had deserved more than just a single day. That much was certain. But even though exhausted afterward, I was thrilled to have at least seen countless treasures of the world collected in that wonderful museum.

A warm, sunny afternoon sharing the broad sidewalk and bench with hundreds of pigeons beside the River Seine, gazing over toward the Notre Dame Cathedral, caused me to revel in my good fortune of being alive in Paris, if only for a very short visit, and made me feel like I was part of a very special place in the world.

So did the walk to the Left Bank in the Latin Quarter to view Sorbonne University and the sidewalk cafes that remained from the old Parisian Bohemian days and still served as a hangout for university students and artists. The area oozed with a sense of the avant-garde, where people, young and old alike, gathered for coffee and what appeared to be French pastries being consumed at mid-day. They were most likely exchanging all their artistic ideas and exuding their pure brightness all the way around. I did not trespass there for very long, sensing that my attire and haircut made me stand out as an American GI surrounded by hip and most likely anti-war Frenchmen. I wandered on, knowing that I really did not fit in their world.

There was still time for taking in the Eiffel Tower later in the evening to view that magnificent and glowing cultural site where marriage proposals are so often made. Is it really any wonder that Paris is called both the City of Light and the City of Love?

On the final day for touring Paris, a walk from the Arc de Triomphe up and then down the Champs Elysees past the tony shops really put things in perspective for me. How was it possible? How could anyone ever afford the merchandise on display? This young $5 a day kid could only dream of such luxuries!

7

It was a long way down to Barcelona from Paris, so the overnight train ride departing at 10 PM would be appropriate for reaching Spain about 2 hours before noon the following day. Unfortunately, some views of the south of France and the Pyrenees mountains would have to be missed in the darkness, but it made sense to travel by night to save an entire day on the travel calendar. The 30-day clock was ticking; a single day was worth saving.

After climbing down from the train, I stood holding the suitcase in my left hand and my guidebook in the other, looking for an available taxi to take me to the exact area where the recommended hotel would be.

The room on the street side proved to be perfect, complete with a small wrought iron walk-out balcony overlooking La Rambla below. Eager to start mingling with the crowds already strolling on the pedestrian boulevard, I began an earnest search for a place to grab something for lunch.

Every little side street, or rambla, seemed lined with restaurants, but they were all closed until lunch that wouldn't officially begin until 2 PM. What? My watch showed that it was almost noon, and I was extremely hungry. It became painfully clear that this strange mealtime and siesta rhythm of Spain would certainly take some getting used to. Finally locating a small cafe that was still open from the mid-morning snack time, I ordered a frittata. It was so good that I could have easily eaten another, but there was too much exploring to be done on this beginning day in Spain to be overly stuffed.

After lunch I quickly boarded a train for the long ride north to visit La Sagrada Familia, the massive but still unfinished basilica by the famous Spanish architect Antoni Gaudi. A classic example of his Gothic work, scarcely a straight line or right angle could be found anywhere on the cathedral while viewing it through the window of the approaching train. And while still blocks away, the circular spires atop the basilica were visible as they reached high into the heavens.

While ascending an outside stairway that wrapped around the curving whitewashed walls likely made of sandstone, I noticed small, irregularly shaped pieces of brightly colored pottery randomly imbedded into the walls. They did not seem to represent any mosaic pattern, though, unlike thousands in use elsewhere throughout the edifice. Was it the irregular shape or the random spacing of the shards that offended me? I sensed that they were totally out of place and even somewhat gaudy, but just who was I, really, to make any judgement whatsoever on his artistic penchant for uniqueness?

The return ride down to Las Ramblas arrived just as the restaurants were finally opening their doors for dinner at exactly 10 PM. Window after window had the evening's menu on full display, with bowls filled with many types of vegetables and fruits and platters of meats and even plated desserts. But in the center of every display rested a huge round metal skillet of seafood paella, long considered by many Spaniards and practically every tourist to be the national dish of Spain. Without fail, I had a plate of saffron-infused paella each night for dinner!

Why had I even bothered to travel to the beach area south of the city, anyway? Sure, the Mediterranean waters were probably irresistibly warm, which had no doubt brought all the beachgoers swarming down from Barcelona proper on this Saturday morning in November. But I had no business being there.

The beach was crowded with families and couples. Children laughed and shrieked as they frolicked in the shallow water amid tiny waves at the very edge of the sea under the watchful eyes of their mothers who were sitting up on the dry sand beneath colorful umbrellas of yellow or blue and even brilliant green and white stripes. Young couples strolled barefoot while holding hands, and many others just enjoyed sunbathing side by side. The lifeguards perched up in their stands were keeping watch over groups of 2 or 3 who were swimming out in the deep water.

I had no business whatsoever being there. None. My clothing was certainly not beachwear. And I wouldn't be caught dead strolling around barefoot with my trousers rolled up, revealing those milky white legs while stepping into the sea to feel the Mediterranean water. This was not going to happen, that much was for sure! And besides, I couldn't even swim, so what business did I really have there?

The return train back to Barcelona was noteworthy for being very slow with the passenger car swaying, almost wobbling, on the narrow track. This slice of the interior of Spain, while only about 40 or so miles out from the actual city, produced a comparison to very early train travel throughout the Old West as depicted in American western movies.

Arriving back at the hotel room around dusk, I sat out on the balcony and leaned forward at the railing to watch the steady stream of mostly young couples moving in the crowd beneath the streetlamps. They sauntered down the right side of the boulevard to where it ended near the Columbus Monument at the very edge of the Mediterranean Sea before turning back around and strolling right back up on the other side. Soft voices and seemingly idle chatter filtered up to the balcony where I sat, indistinguishable but very pleasant sounds that left me straining to catch any Spanish words or phrases that I could decipher.

This movement of couples resembled a slow dance, a ritual being carried out by actors on this Saturday night on the broad promenade below me, much like an ancient rite of passage for young lovers who were totally oblivious to my presence and observation of them from overhead.

Deep melancholy had already overtaken me by the time I retreated into the now-darkened hotel room and searched around for the wall light switch. I had lingered out on that balcony perch too long. Way too long. But it wasn't just that ebb and flow of those strollers down on La Rambla that had triggered this overwhelming feeling of aloneness on this Saturday evening, since that longing for companionship had already crept in earlier while walking around down at the beach. Assuring myself that I would return after the war to these same locations, returning someday with my own girl at my side, did little if anything at this moment to settle my very deep sense of not belonging, of not really belonging anywhere at all.

"Well, just snap out of it!" That was sage advice from others who had already passed this way before, and I was determined to follow it. Besides, dinnertime was fast approaching. I was hungry, and yet another

steaming plate of Spanish seafood paella would soon
be my personal reward!

8

For the most economical travel, one should probably use only local transit as often as possible for simply getting from one place to another. Everybody knows this, of course, but this time that maxim had been carried out just a bit too far.

On yet another train, the 2nd of 4 transfers necessary to reach the capitol city of Rome, my train seat was forward-facing and about midway back in the car. No window seat had been available on the right side, but locals knew that there would not be a view of the sea anyway, not during this leg of the journey along the bottom of France before finally reaching the Italian border after Monaco. Although the train did stop at the station, it did not appear that anyone got off, at least not from my car, to join the scene at the famous Monte Carlo Casino in that enclave of astonishing wealth that made up the tiny Principality of Monaco. Several passengers did board, however, filling up any remaining seats. Two were up ahead of me on the left and seemed to know each other. By their attire it appeared that they might well have been the hourly staff that had just finished their shift at the stores that make up the shopping district. The young ladies had settled into their seats and chatted for several minutes before napping as the train rumbled on.

Night had fallen, so even if that coveted window seat had been mine, the sea would have been too dark to enjoy the view, anyway. The dome lights were all lit, so it was the middle-aged woman sitting next to me on my right and her traveling companions who were facing us, a grandmother next to a teenaged girl, who had now gained my attention. The 3 had been in non-stop conversation ever since boarding at the station just a few miles short of the Italian border crossing. Their language did sound a little familiar. It wasn't Spanish, was it? Maybe it was Basque or maybe even Italian, but it certainly wasn't something that I could recognize.

They had boarded the coastal train to travel toward some destination further down in Italy. Their layered clothing was topped off with heavy overcoats, and large purses and cloth bags were piled on their laps. Clustered near their feet were mismatched luggage pieces and 1 battered cardboard box with a blanket draped over it that the girl periodically peeked into. And it was from this box that I detected some sort of foul odor as well as the sound of scratching, as if a pet wanted out to join them.

Their highly animated speech had actually sounded somewhat like Spanish, the single foreign language that I could haltingly use, so I decided to try on a little conversation with the lady seated beside me.

"Habla usted Español o Ingles?"

Her response was easy to understand, as she smiled and simply said,

"No."

Even her next phrase was clear to me when she said,

"Io parlo Italiano."

That was it! It had been the Italian language all along. Our conversation managed to fumble along while I used Spanish and she Italian, and to our amazement we were able to communicate on a rudimentary level by the unbelievable similarities in words and sounds and phrases between the 2 Romance languages. All the while, the grandmother sat in the seat facing me with a smile plastered all over her face and just kept nodding at me. The young teenager, though, seemed very shy and tended to avoid any direct eye contact. Besides, her preoccupation was with whatever live creature was hiding in that cardboard box at her feet.

Yes, I was by myself and traveling around Europe for an adventure. I had already visited Germany, France, and Spain, but had not been through the mountain village where they had just spent the last week. Yes, I was a soldier in the U.S. Army. I then learned that her 2 sons were military men as well, both currently serving in the Italian Navy. And her daughter, Aurora, had just turned 14.

Finally, my curiosity just had to be satisfied. Without a clue how to ask what was in the cardboard box, I pointed down to it before raising my hands as if to ask, "What's in there?" Now the teen girl came alive! She eagerly uncovered the box containing 7 young pullets, all white, and all scratching away at the straw while looking for feed. Aurora beamed with pride at her clandestine little brood of chickens as her mother explained that they were all to be sold somewhere further down the line.

At least in Italy, this is what journeying by local transit *really* meant!

"Colosseum, please." The taxi then headed off in the general direction of that ruin that I really wanted to see right away. While Rome presented many sights to take in during the 4 allotted days, none compared to seeing the place where so many Christians had been fed to those ravenously hungry lions or where young gladiators had fought each other to an awful death while 1000s of spectators egged them on from seats above.

The steep angle of the stone steps and seats had provided attendees at those weekly sporting events an incredible view of the carnage and battles below. I could almost hear the roar from the crowds of 2000 years ago, but only for a fleeting moment. All those blood-thirsty Romans were long gone now, replaced by scores of feral cats that silently slinked around the stands, first emerging from underneath the decayed stairways and seats before disappearing again into the caverns below. In my imagination, I viewed these cats as the miniature descendants of all the lions that had enjoyed those feeding frenzies so very, very long ago. Weren't they? I wondered.

It was a pleasantly warm day in Rome, a weekday perfectly suited for strolling around the grounds of what remained of the Roman Forum. Time seemed to be standing still among the ruins; there was no sense of busyness or rush on this particular Tuesday afternoon. The quiet and peacefulness of this broad, cobblestone-floored space was disturbed only by a little boy who giggled and skipped and ran along as he kept getting further ahead of his grandparents. Several people could be seen viewing the buildings and all the scattered remnants over on Palatine Hill, while still others moved among the stately trees at the edge of the grounds. Otherwise, it appeared that I had the place largely to myself as I meandered and circled around to gain various angles to study the tall pillars that had once supported the grand porches of the ancient Temple of Saturn. Other structures lay in ruins, where lawyers and senators with their aides had no doubt entered and exited every day as they carried out the affairs of state all those ages ago.

But it wasn't just the columns that were tall; ancient oaks reached for the sky as did the umbrella-topped stone pines that have forever served to define the Forum grounds.

Evening was now rapidly approaching as I rested on a north-facing bench to soak in the ancient history that surrounded me. Off to the west, the last of the sunshine was producing an indescribable color in the cloudless sky. Was that a faded pink or did it change to rose mixed in with ever-so-pale lavender? Without any question at all, it was God's paintbrush serving as the nightcap to a glorious Roman day.

Since my lodging was in the central part of the city, the remaining places to visit were all within walking distance of each other. Some locations were a couple of miles apart, but I was young and certainly in the best shape of my life, so I knew that I could manage every distance well enough before ending each day in happy exhaustion.

Starting the next day with a brisk walk over to St. Peter's Square, I gave a quick glance up to the high balcony from which those papal appearances were made before heading straight over to the Vatican to purchase a ticket to view the various museums and, most importantly, the beautiful Sistine Chapel with Michelangelo's frescoes on full display, including the famous ceiling painting that depicted Adam being created by the finger of God.

"Chicago pizza started right here in Italy, in Rome," the salesman proclaimed in heavily accented English from behind the cash register of the small shop. But not wishing to argue such things with him, I wolfed down the enormous slice of deep-dish cheese pizza and pretended to like it despite the excessive dough. In fact, only the bottle of cold Coke was memorable.

With still over a mile of walking to go before reaching the Spanish Steps and the Tivoli Fountains, I stopped for a rest on a sunlit bench. Was it that pizza dough that was making me feel sluggish at midday? Maybe all I needed was another Coca-Cola.

The monotonous and high-pitched voice of the tour bus driver's proclamations being delivered over the loudspeaker announced the arrival of the enormous green bus which had stopped directly in front of my position beside the flowing fountains and disgorged 20 American couples, all dressed in polyester leisure wear. Each person sported a large sun hat and dark sunglasses to complete the full tourist look. Scarcely even glancing over at the many beautiful fountains or even listening to the rushing water, most of them seemed much more intent on aligning themselves for the perfect camera shot to gush over when they all returned home. There they would undoubtedly bore everyone with endless pictures that meant precious little to their viewers and barely anything to them as well, since they, themselves, had not really bothered to absorb much of the surroundings that made up tourist Stop # 5 on the daylong bus tour of Rome.

Right then and there, I vowed to never be one of those travelers. Never. Not even in old age!

On the early morning train to Florence, I kept looking out the left-sided window as Rome faded away in the distance, remembering back to the impressions and images that had made the visit so enjoyable.

I reflected on the Roman sunsets that were so very spectacular every evening, most often enjoyed from my own west-facing balcony. I recalled heading down to the hotel dining room each dinnertime and being seated alone at a table for 2 that was always draped in a white tablecloth with a single red carnation in the center and being served a full 3-course Italian dinner complete with a glass of complimentary house wine on what was called the American Plan.

My extensive walks around the city had led to central plazas serving as gathering places for the inhabitants of apartment buildings that surrounded them, where elderly men sat on wrought iron chairs at little café tables passing the midday hours away while reading newspapers. Women called out to each other from the windows above as they hung laundry items out to dry on clothes lines operated by primitive pulley systems that crossed over to the next building from high above the streets.

The old men had their newspapers, but the young men had their reputations to defend. Known for their flirtatious ways on the streets of Rome, young ladies walking along on the sidewalks, even in small groups, always seemed to draw the attention of these men. On several occasions, I actually witnessed 3 or 4 guys run across the street to greet the young women—mostly blond ones—in a manner that some might call harassment or even assault. How was it possible that the ladies might enjoy such in-your-face attention?

My time in Italy was quickly ending, but there was no way in this world that I intended to miss getting off the train in Florence to view Michelangelo's statue of

David inside the Uffizi Museum. Rounding a corner, I walked inside and there he stood in gleaming white marble, fully illuminated by a skylight, and rising a full 17 feet from the gallery floor. I was truly stunned—totally overwhelmed! As I approached the statue for a closer look, the examination revealed the figure's athleticism, near-exact anatomy and, clutched in his left hand, the sling that would be used to slay Goliath in that famous biblical account.

The sculptor Michelangelo, at just 23 years of age, had shown to the world his absolute genius at such a tender age.

The Leaning Tower of Pisa was visible way off in the distance from the left side of the train. I focused on the building as long as possible before it slipped out of view, mentally documenting that it indeed had a significant lean to the right.

9

The Netherlands now beckoned to me, loudly calling out my name.

Because the train would travel throughout the night and require more than 15 hours, I had resigned to try and sleep in my seat as much as possible. Still, when the journey finally ended at the Amsterdam Centraal, I detrained in a thoroughly exhausted state, stiff and hungry and needing to secure a hotel room.

And what a cute hotel it turned out to be. Yes, it was selected from the trusted $5 A Day guidebook, but who could have predicted that the front would have leaned out over a canal and that the interior would have incredibly steep wooden stairs with no elevator up to the 4th floor room? I was very tired, and the tiny bed was entirely welcoming. My sleep that night was sound, so sound that I nearly missed breakfast the next morning. Not that I would have really missed all that much—nothing was offered but cold cuts and cold bread. I reminded myself that the meager fare was included in the dirt-cheap hotel rate; I should be grateful. Besides, there was lunchtime to anticipate.

How was it possible to have such gorgeous tulips this late in November? They were everywhere, displayed in full glory on canal overpasses and along sidewalks, mixed in with other flowers offered for purchase.

Even the bicycles bunched up in racks nearby were painted in inviting colors and were being rented for a ride through the Vondelpark, a large, beautiful park set right in the middle of the shopping district and surrounded by high rise office buildings. I chose to sit and watch people as they passed by. Tourists were still everywhere, even this late in the year, and the place was crawling with hippies who had converged on this old Dutch city to revel in the lax enforcement of drug laws. Whiffs of burning marijuana floated on the air from time to time, but nobody cared. This was Amsterdam in 1970.

Rembrandt's paintings, along with some works from Vincent van Gogh and various Dutch Masters, filled the Rijksmuseum, which demanded 6 hours to fully appreciate everything on display. It had been a slow, leisurely stroll from my hotel along the canal-lined streets over to the vast museum. Along the way I had spotted a perfect little café to have a sidewalk meal afterward. But that outside spot was not to be mine. Instead, my table was tucked inside the dark interior, since only couples and a few foursomes had already claimed every table in the late afternoon sunshine by the time of my return. But that wonderful plateful of shrimp pasta more than compensated for the lesser table. And besides, my spot inside was right next to the dessert display case, allowing me to drool over that large slice of lemon cake long before it ended up being placed before me.

10

Only London remained on my Grand Tour of Europe; it would be the final 2 days on the continent. Where, oh where had all the time gone, anyway? At least my cash money hadn't totally dried up. Before departing Amsterdam, I had carefully counted every dollar and determined that there was plenty of wiggle room for a little splurge on a sleeper seat. Oh, how very sweet it would be to arrive in England and to be totally fresh and well rested.

By the time the large, ship-sized ferry started backing away from the dock in Rotterdam for the overnight sea voyage to London, everyone had already selected food items from the cafeteria line and was seated at tables in the dining room.

I was feeling exceptionally smug as I started in on the salad smothered with blue cheese dressing. After all, this budget traveler would be making that crossing in the coveted First-Class sleeping section!

It didn't take very long to understand why each table had a rimmed edge all around, just tall enough to catch any sliding plates, utensils, or glasses when the vessel swayed across the water. And that dreadful swaying had already begun. Smooth but relentlessly rhythmic, the ferry was yawning back and forth in the angry swells of the North Sea.

My dinner was ruined. In fact, the entire night was totally ruined. I barely made it to a far corner stall in the restroom before losing it all and literally spending the entire 6-hour night voyage huddled in the same stall, dry heaving hour after endless hour. So much for splurging on a Sleeper Chair!

Finally emerging from the tiny London hotel room where I'd slept the entire day away, I gingerly walked the already-dark street and stopped at a newsstand to purchase the local paper. But what language was the newspaperman speaking? It sure didn't sound like English. Was his accent that heavy that I couldn't even decipher a single word? Having no idea what he had quoted for the price, except to catch the word shillings, I handed over the largest denomination of a pound note that I had, hoping against hope that he would return the appropriate change.

I found a little eating place that served a thin soup and, once again, ice-cold bread. Only sipping on the soup, I managed to keep it down. Happy to be feeling better, I slowly made my way back to the hotel and read every page of that newspaper before hitting the bed to sleep through the night.

London! The list of places to see and things to do was long. Many locations would be within easy walking distance of each other, but I intended to start making use of those red double-decker buses when needed.

To begin, I joined other ticketholders for the tour of Westminster Abbey where we followed behind the guide who spoke in rather hushed tones inside the dimly lit church ringed by stained-glass windows very high up on the walls above. After he pointed up to a large window that had more light streaming through it than the others, he declared, "This is Westminster Abbey's exquisite and world-famous Rose Window."

Luckily it was Sunday, so I departed the Abbey and the huge bell that is called Big Ben and headed over toward Buckingham Palace for the Changing of the Guards. And what an elegant display of precision! The procedure was truly steeped in authentic British tradition, and I loved it.

Speakers' Corner at the east end of Hyde Park was something I had read about and wanted to see for myself. Each Sunday for generations, anyone could rig a soapbox to stand on and speak about anything at all in an informal, mostly ad lib fashion. On this particular day a very young Caucasian man, dressed in a peculiar brown robe that flowed to the top of his sneakers and wearing blond dreadlocks, was ranting on and on in his British accent about the pure evil of apartheid down in South Africa.

At the hotel dining room on Monday morning, the waitress informed me that the breakfast would be an American-style meal. Oh, really? I must have beamed at that good news! Her only question was whether I'd prefer my eggs to be scrambled, fried, or poached.

The plate arrived with 2 scrambled eggs, 3 long strips of bacon, and bread slices that had been toasted with orange marmalade covering each piece. But there was something wrong. Something was very wrong with the bacon. Each of the 3 strips appeared to be completely raw!

When the meal was completed and the plate picked up, she noticed the untouched bacon and apologized for failing to suggest sausages as an alternate meat choice. I mumbled something about enjoying bacon that's cooked just a bit more, to which she replied, "Oh, here in Great Britain we never burn the bacon the way the Americans do!"

My very last day in Europe was spent just sightseeing around London from the inside of a double-decker bus, traveling to the London Bridge that spanned the River Thames and then over to Trafalgar Square and Nelson's Column and finally to Piccadilly Circus. In the afternoon, I sat up on the front bench on the 2nd level, looking down as a small group of elementary students boarded, dressed in school uniforms that included brown plaid jackets.

All too soon, I had to fetch a little black London cab for the ride out to Heathrow Airport. Sadly, my tour was over. However, a brand-new thrill awaited. The plane for crossing the pond to New York was a huge Boeing 747, complete with tons of legroom in coach, a complete dinner with a cloth napkin, and Charlton Heston's new film, Ben Hur, as the full-length movie afterwards.

With no time to tarry in NYC, I made my connection out to Anchorage. From my window seat, it became obvious why Alaska is labeled as our largest state. We flew over miles of snow-covered mountains, snow so thick that nothing but white could be seen. This went on for hours, literally hours. It's a very big state, all right!

Then it was time for landing. I could see nothing but white on the runway, which terrified me. Would we be landing on packed snow or ice? Whew! I was very glad to be on the ground at long last and still in one piece.

Saigon was next! It would require 3 different Pan Am jets from Anchorage to Southeast Asia to complete this full circumnavigation of the globe, but I would be reporting to my new duty station at 3rd Field Hospital before the week was over.

Has anyone heard of a 30-day Grand Tour of Europe on a meager $5 daily budget?

If only you knew.

A PLEA FOR PLAYMATES

By the time we reached the pullout on the downhill roadway, long shadows were already darkening the mountainside. Sunlight still shone here and there in small patches on the downslope below us, but even that would be gone within half an hour.

A report that a heavy snowstorm had finally hit the mountains at Frazier Park was the trigger that sent us out from Simi Valley on our road trip that Saturday morning. Both Paul and Ryan had stashed their round bright orange saucer sleds in the van for a full day of endlessly sledding down the snow-covered runs up on the mountain.

Other families shared the sledding area, and the cold air was always filled with loud shrieks of excitement and even occasional screams of pain when someone lost control and ran into an exposed rock or brushed against a tree trunk in the freefall tumble behind or often out in front of an escaping sled.

Today had been no different. After hours of sledding, half-frozen and very hungry, we trudged back up the steep hill to the parked van to find warmth and food. When the inside of the van had finally warmed up, we inhaled the Albertson's deli sandwiches and the Little Debbie snack cakes, then washed them down with our Dr. Pepper sodas.

Before driving back down the mountain toward our home, it was determined that I would need to devise some sort of dressing to cover up the slight abrasion on Ryan's left palm. A Band Aid here and there—each overlapping the other—did the trick.

Just a few miles into the drive down the mountain, I heard the boys, almost in perfect unison, say,

"Dad, we forgot to get any pinecones!"

Oops. That would not be okay at all, since the huge cardboard box in the garage was not yet completely full.

"Ok, I'll stop as soon as I can find a turnout. But let's make it quick. I don't want to freeze all over again."

The air was cold and got even colder when a slight breeze began to stir down in the pine branches just below us. But since pinecones covered the ground at the pullout beside the road, our job of tossing them into the back of the van was quickly accomplished.

As the tailgate was closing, we heard it—a haunting, pleading sound from young voices floating up from somewhere down the slope. We each turned toward the voices and spotted the place they were coming from. A wide beam of sunlight was still shining on a small wooden cabin mostly hidden among the trees. Standing out on the deck and gazing up toward the roadside some 300 yards above them were a young girl all bundled up in a pink winter coat and a slightly younger boy dressed in blue jeans and a black jacket. Then we heard their pleading voices again,

"Come back! We want to play with you!"

As we moved to get into the van, we heard them a final time,

"Come back! We want to play with you!"

Stunned into silence, we drove away. As we headed down out of the mountains for our home nearly 75 miles away, we each felt a very deep sense of pity for those lonely children and briefly discussed what we might have done differently if we'd had more time.

Before too long, though, the boys had drifted off into deep, exhausted sleep to the sounds of "La Vida" by Sandy Owen, dreaming of their fun-filled adventure on those Southern California snowbanks.

THE LETTER OF INQUIRY

1

The usual ritual began when the mail was sorted that evening. Bills along with legitimate correspondence were stacked together for review while any obvious junk mail and all circulars were immediately tossed into the wastebasket. And such was the case with the official letter mailed straight out of Sacramento from the CA Board of Registered Nursing. It was not license renewal time, so why was my name on the envelope?

Inside this envelope was a single folded sheet with the BRN letterhead across the top and a beginning paragraph that was an apology for both the intrusion and the probing questions that followed. By the final paragraph it had become clear why an apology had been offered from the start. There certainly was an attempted intrusion into my life from an unnamed person who was trying hard to track down someone from the distant past, an intruder who was going to great lengths to locate me strictly based on a hunch that the Board could verify that I lived in California and had a license issued by that state.

Each question gave me an immediate sense that the answers were already well known. "Was I originally from New Mexico? Had I been in the Army in 1969-1970? Had I been a medic serving in Vietnam during the war? If all the answers are affirmative, may the

Board please exercise the liberty to share my contact information with the unnamed inquirer?"

2

Gazing out at the long air strip bathed in morning sunlight, one could only guess at the temperature of the outside air as we hurriedly descended onto the runway at Cam Rahn Bay and taxied toward the small wooden building that served as the terminal. Every soldier onboard that seemingly endless flight across the Pacific had undoubtedly heard something about the excessively hot climate of South Vietnam, along with other accounts and rumors and warnings about what we could expect during our time in-country. But only those individuals returning for another voluntary tour of duty in Asia really knew if any of that chatter was even true.

Since I was seated very near the front of the plane, I was among those who would feel the heat that came rushing into the cabin when the door swung open. But it was on the stairs going down to the tarmac where it hit me squarely in the face, an oppressive wall of humidity and 100-degree heat on this early December morning. This was awful! Just awful! And to think that this was to be the new normal for an entire year in this war-torn country.

We were now on the ground in Southeast Asia, and I couldn't help but wonder if pretty much every other guy had the same thoughts running through his mind as I did, thoughts about how fate and just plain bad luck had converged to drop us off in this place. They all knew, like I did, that some of us would never see our hometowns or families again.

First impressions very often last and become forever memories, and not one of us who endured the insults hurled directly at us as we stood in the noon chow line under that broiling sun would ever be able to forget any of it.

On our left, a moving column of soldiers was passing by in the opposite direction on their way to board the bus that would take them over to the waiting Boeing 707 for their long journey back home, back to the "World" that we had all just left behind. Their jungle fatigues were faded to a lighter green than the dark color of our newly issued uniforms, and their boots seemed very worn and encrusted with dried reddish mud. Every man's face was deeply suntanned and hardened, but we did notice that a few of the men still managed to wear expressions of hope, knowing that their freedom bird would soon lift off. Yet several of them felt a need to snicker and ridicule us as they passed by, calling out, "Look at those FNGs!" We all just recoiled inside, somehow knowing that brand new recruits and what they had snarled at us went hand in hand. "Freakin' new guys! You'd better watch out, newbies. VC are everywhere!"

After finally arriving at LZ Schueller, the landing zone up in the Central Highlands, I anxiously awaited the arrival of the new medic who would share my bunker. Details were very scarce about what circumstances had required a replacement medic to begin with. My master sergeant was unwilling to discuss it with me, and I soon learned that too many probing questions during wartime are never appropriate.

And there he stood just inside the aid station door. He was an 18-year-old man with thick, dark brown hair, Army-issued glasses and boyish good looks with his right hand extended to greet me, wearing a broad smile that was almost a grin as he stated his name. While still shaking hands, he asked,

"Doc, when is chow? I'm starving! The ride up here from Pleiku in that old deuce and a half took forever. I thought we'd never get here!"

Sitting together in the tin-roofed mess hall, everyone lingered for a while over introductions, and we found that conversation with him came easy. He was from Indiana and made an immediate bond with another medic from the Hoosier state. Having never traveled west of the Mississippi, he expressed great interest in what it must really be like out in the wilds of my home state of New Mexico, asking in a lighthearted way if it was still part of Old Mexico.

The months slowly passed by as each of us adjusted to being participants in a war so far away from our hometowns. During the routine of working together in the aid station, I came to know this new medic as a quiet and generally soft-spoken young man from a conservative background, a person with a deeply held sense of right and wrong that stemmed from his early Christian upbringing, a sense so strong that he really could not be shaken even when prodded for debate or ridiculed for his beliefs. It was quite noticeable that he displayed a genuine acceptance of others without ever making any judgements whatsoever. There was a rather perpetual cheerfulness about him that was sometimes contagious. And even though everyone on the entire landing zone referred to me as "Doc," I was particularly aware of this person's unfeigned respect for my position as the senior corpsman.

Seemingly endless days were passed with him in the aid station out at LZ Schueller. Between patients and other interruptions, like the clap of outgoing artillery or that unmistakable whistle of incoming rockets, we shared our stories and talked about everything under the sun and read whatever we could get our hands on, which was never much. While I had inherited an odd assortment of paperbacks shelved in a makeshift bookcase fashioned from a wooden ammo box, the pickings were very slim. But one novel really did grab our attention, something titled "One Flew Over the Cuckoo's Nest." We took turns reading that book, recalling Army battle axes we had known during our training who reminded us of Nurse Ratched!

When the day arrived for me to depart LZ Schueller for my new duty station at the hospital down-country in Saigon, we all exchanged handshakes and warm goodbyes but, as was the practice among departing soldiers in war zones, did not share real information or addresses for any further personal contact back in the World. That just wasn't done. We literally viewed everything and everybody in the immediate moment, only in real time, rather than with plans for any future connection stateside. No. It just wasn't done.

3

The letter finally arrived in June with the late evening mail. Who could have sent it? The envelope bore no return address and was postmarked from some zip code back in North Carolina. My complete name and address had been carefully written with blue ink in handwriting that I didn't recognize. And I didn't know a single person from that state. So, who was this?

While awaiting the eventual arrival of this mysterious letter, I had spent considerable time pondering who would emerge as the person from many decades ago who had gone to great lengths to locate me. My mind had searched all the way back to those long-ago days in Vietnam, considering friends and even those I had known only casually.

Would it be the captain? Just maybe. That would be something he might do. But he was Texas born and bred, and everybody knows Texans don't generally move to the Carolinas. Then there was my best friend from Basic Training who had been sent to the war zone as well. That one was a good guess, I thought, since we had been so close as unwilling draftees. There were a few other medics to consider, two in particular, but they were both from the Midwest and not likely to have relocated after the war. And the physician who had been drafted just like most of the rest of us, so awkwardly serving in wartime as the medical director when his specialty was psychiatry, really seemed to be a logical choice. He and I had had many wonderful conversations and genuinely liked each other's company, but it didn't seem too likely that he would leave Chicago where his practice had been so successful to end up in North Carolina.

Finally, I was sure I'd figured it out. It was the female RN. Absolutely! After all, she came from over on the coast in Monterey. We had been such great friends in Saigon, spending all scheduled days off from the hospital together, riding in that vast sea of bicycles and motorcycles through the streets of Saigon on my little Honda 90 motorcycle. Oh, what a spectacle we must have made—two American soldiers in our Army uniforms astride that tiny red bike, weaving our way toward the outskirts of the city to travel throughout the countryside on those narrow blacktop highways. She had volunteered to be an Army nurse and was thrilled to be assigned to the hospital in Saigon. We had shared a wonderful sense of adventure together. Yes. It had to be her!

My anticipation was quite high when I sat down to open the letter. Who was it going to be?

The answer flabbergasted me when I read his name. It was the young replacement medic who had shared my bunker way out at LZ Schueller all those ages ago!

The Indiana boy had transplanted himself to North Carolina, apparently, and wanted to reconnect after so many, many years.

Thrilled beyond belief, I grabbed my phone and hit the numbers listed on the page. Just before it started to ring, my wife called out, "Wait! It's 3 hours later back there. He's already asleep!" I quickly touched the hang-up button and let out a sigh. What kind of hideous impression would that have made on my old buddy, my good friend from way over on the other side of the world all those years ago?

He had obviously made it out of Vietnam, too, and I was anxious to talk with him just as soon as possible.

My sleep was fitful as I waited for Saturday morning to hit the East Coast, but I woke at my usual time of 0330 anyway. Supposing he would most likely be at home, I dialed in the call precisely 30 minutes later. The phone just kept ringing and ringing and ringing on his end, making me momentarily wonder if I had used the correct number. Just when I was about to hang up, a groggy voice mumbled, "Hello?"

Oh joy, I had just succeeded in making the grandest of all hideous impressions after all!

"Hey, Doc! I finally found you!"

There was no mistaking the enthusiasm in that still familiar-sounding voice!

Our conversation went on a long time that morning as we gradually got caught up on the many decades that had already passed. He had married soon upon return from the war in Vietnam, but his marriage had ended in divorce many years earlier, exactly like the experience of almost all Vietnam veterans. But there wasn't the slightest trace of acrimony or blame as he discussed the end of his marriage, making it apparent that he was still very good at accepting people and situations without making any judgements. Nope. No change whatsoever there!

In my eagerness to rendezvous with him, I offered to stop by the following month for an hour-long visit, since I would be driving past his small town around 11 PM to catch an early morning flight back to LA. My attendance at a conference in Winston-Salem would end on that night and the freeway would run right past his location. He readily agreed and told me to find him by a red F-150 pickup at the 24-hour Waffle House restaurant by the only off-ramp for the town.

4

Cruising through the nearly full, dimly lit parking lot, my headlights picked up a figure seated on an open tailgate, dressed in jeans with an untucked shirt and a blue baseball cap, attire that seemed to be quite appropriate for such a sultry summer night down in the South. I immediately stopped the sedan without seeking a parking space, leaving the bright headlights shining directly on this person. As he stared into the headlights there seemed to be a touch of something that I recognized, but I couldn't quite place it. Was it his eyes? More likely, was it the familiar way he sat on the tailgate, leaning forward with elbows on his knees and hands loosely clasped? Maybe that was it.

Finally stepping out of the car, I approached him and asked,

"Hey, is that you?"

We looked at each other for several seconds in the brightness of the headlights before a slow grin began to spread across both of our faces. We greeted each other with a handshake, avoiding what would have been an awkward hug in the middle of the parking lot with diners heading back to their cars. Besides, both of us had apparently retained our feeling of reserve borne from distinct individual personalities as well as from discipline acquired during our military training. Nope, no change whatsoever there, either!

Sitting at a small booth next to a darkened window just inside the doorway, we studied each other in the bright lights of the diner. To my surprise, he hadn't aged much at all. He still had a full head of brown hair without any sign of gray at the temples. He no longer had the same youthful face from decades earlier, of course, but he had retained the same handsomeness and was as trim and fit as he had been way back then.

Over hot coffee and slices of lemon meringue pie, we both poured over the pictures in the albums he had brought into the restaurant. I couldn't get enough of them! Because I had no pictures at all to document my experiences in-country, viewing his photographs that showed the way we were and what we did found me looking long and hard at them. And his memory was quite remarkable, remembering the names of all the guys and identifying the location for every scene.

While the photographs generally depicted only good memories, we commented on the genuine sadness felt over those who had ultimately been lost forever and the ones that he had been unable to keep track of after I left the Central Highlands for Saigon.

Eventually, while examining my tie and suit jacket, he asked,

"So, what was this conference up there in Winston-Salem all about?"

I told him it had been a full week of sermons from Baptist preachers just like an old-fashioned revival. My reply surprised him since he had only known me as an avowed agnostic with a penchant for debate and even mockery of Christianity. I informed him that my pastor had led me to saving faith in Christ in the early 1990s and that everything had really changed from that point on. He quickly mumbled something about having to wait and see about that, but it was said with a big smile on his face.

Just a few hours later I was in the air heading back to California, reliving every minute of the time we had spent together. We had promised to keep in touch, so I started making plans for the next summer.

The gathering took place at my son's farm in Virginia over a July 4th weekend the following summer, with Texas brisket and Brazos Bottom pecan pies shipped in from Houston along with all the usual trimmings, including Low Country Southern-style potato salad and hand-made apple pies fresh from the oven. The North Carolina veteran seemed to thoroughly enjoy the outing and cracked up from time to time from the antics of one of my grandsons as the toddler played with the other children inside the farmhouse.

Earlier that morning in the quietness out in the living room beside the huge picture window framing the pastoral view, he had listened intently as my younger son, a senior pastor from San Francisco, had shared Scripture that gave him an assurance of salvation in Christ that he had never really known before.

Two old buddies from Vietnam. Two brand new men now in Christ. Had he changed? Had I changed? The spiritual change for both of us was truly enormous and deepened a full half-century of now-rekindled friendship that will endure forever.

With the single exception of a military reunion out in Colorado years earlier, where his hotel window gave him a head-on view of Pikes Peak itself, he has still never traveled west of the Mississippi. Well, at least he's not been west of the Rockies! He's been actively shying far away from the West Coast his whole life, regarding California as the "Land of Fruits and Nuts" and maintaining that he really would go completely bonkers "parked" on the LA freeways. But despite all my assurances that I would handle every bit of the driving, he has steadfastly declined every invitation to venture out this far west. I'm still working on him!

SADDLEBAG TREASURES

1

By the early 1900s, almost every ranch hand working the spreads below Colorado's Front Range already knew about those special treats that the womenfolk would always add, 2 in each saddlebag, that helped the cowboys get through those long workdays out on the open rangeland, the summertime days that could last every bit of 10 hours and sometimes even longer.

The cowboys would be in their saddles and ready to ride out after an early breakfast of fresh coffee along with heaping platters of eggs, thick sausage patties, and fried potatoes served with piping hot browned biscuits slathered with freshly churned butter. It was a meal worthy to be called a real ranch breakfast.

They would ride the endless fence lines in search of stray cattle and leaning posts with downed barbed wire, not returning to enter the ranch house at day's end until all the animals were corralled and fed. After washing up at the communal outdoor wash basin by the back door, they would hurry around to the front porch to beat the clanging of the iron bell signifying that supper was ready and on the table.

It wasn't that the noontime meals already packed away in those saddlebags wouldn't be enough food. Every trail rider looked forward to unwrapping a thin off-white kitchen towel to pull out thick slabs of cold ham or steak and huge wedges of cornbread for what was known as dinner, especially when a couple of red apples were included that had been shipped in from the fruit orchards over in Canon City. But it was that morning stretch between breakfast and dinner along around 10 AM and then again about 3 o'clock in the afternoon when every cowboy just seemed to need something extra, a boost from a power-packed snack that was delicious and nourishing.

They would regain energy for the hard work ahead after a short rest stop under the shade of welcoming cottonwood trees by a watering hole, pulling from the saddlebag a single but gigantic oatmeal cookie loaded down with ingredients fit for royalty.

This was the cookie that some years later would even make it into the ranch kitchens down south in New Mexico and over into the Panhandle of Texas before finally making it to Arizona and way out to the far, far west, to the golden state called California.

This legendary and delicious treasure became known as the Cowboy Cookie.

2

Any search of the Internet will turn up recipes for what is claimed to be a cowboy cookie, but a quick review of the ingredients and process will reveal that they are not true to the original recipe at all. Some bakers following these counterfeit recipes even dare to use a Splenda blend rather than light brown sugar, others will substitute with English walnuts when the recipe clearly calls for pecans, while the very worst offenders just skip the coconut all together! And the temperature for the oven and the baking times are just scattered all over, with most of these pretenders failing to seriously consider carryover baking at all.

Coming from a very long line of Colorado ranchers who used and very judiciously preserved the original recipe, I quickly point out the impossibility of finding the real deal anywhere these days except through me. One only need ask my granddaughter Danielle to hear it quickly declared that the only "real" Cowboy Cookie is generated right here in my own Southern California kitchen. And unlike seasonal unavailability of certain staples at the turn of the century, namely coconut, every essential ingredient is easily found in all supermarkets across the land, so any skimping on the true recipe is unjustified. There is just no excuse whatsoever!

Making these cookies doesn't require all that much labor, particularly when grandchildren are involved. When she was young, Danielle would stand on a chair next to the center island and add ingredients to the cookie dough and then stir and stir until well mixed, but nowadays, at age 15, she makes her own in her mother's kitchen.

Her spot at the counter has now been taken by her brother, Blake, who just turned 8 and is already tall enough to stand at the counter and work away. And unlike his sister, he has recently decided to totally avoid the mixing spoon. Instead, he heads over to the kitchen sink and thoroughly washes his hands, then proceeds to do all the mixing with both hands. One very sweet side benefit of this method, of course, is getting so much sticky dough on every finger that it puts him into a finger-licking frenzy when the mixing is all done. Blake has figured out the perfect way to enjoy cookie dough in the raw!

3

Legend holds that no western cowboy ever returned from those endless, dusty rides with a single Cowboy Cookie left in his saddlebag. Never once.

And even though saddlebags have been replaced by those gallon-sized plastic zip lock baggies, no Cowboy Cookie has ever made it all the way up to the final destination of modern-day travelers on their "run up the road" in their snazzy new SUVs, either. No, never once.